As the sun dipped behind the hills, Ari's smile faded. His eyes took on a wide, startled look.

"You'd think I'd get used to this—"

His voice turned hoarse as his jacket began to flow, his face to twist and change, his skin to sprout white fur. Within moments a white bear stood roaring before me. The sound sent shivers down to my bones.

Somewhere deep inside I *knew* I ought to run.

Also by Janni Lee Simner
Bones of Faerie
Faerie Winter

∽ THIEF EYES ∽

Janni Lee Simner

BLUEFIRE

Text copyright © 2010 by Janni Lee Simner
Cover art copyright © 2011 by Random House, Inc.

All rights reserved. Published in the United States by Bluefire, an imprint of Random House Children's Books, a division of Random House, Inc., New York. Originally published in hardcover in the United States by Random House Children's Books, New York, in 2010.

Bluefire and the colophon are trademarks of Random House, Inc.

Visit us on the Web! www.randomhouse.com/teens/strangelands

Educators and librarians, for a variety of teaching tools, visit us at www.randomhouse.com/teachers

The Library of Congress has cataloged the hardcover edition of this work as follows:
Simner, Janni Lee.
Thief eyes / Janni Lee Simner. — 1st ed.
p. cm.
Summary: Haley's mother disappeared while on a trip to Iceland, and a year later, when her father takes her there to find out what happened, Haley finds herself deeply involved in an ancient saga that began with her Nordic ancestors.
ISBN 978-0-375-86670-8 (trade) — ISBN 978-0-375-96670-5 (lib. bdg.) —
ISBN 978-0-375-89682-8 (ebook)
[1. Magic—Fiction. 2. Folklore—Iceland—Fiction.
3. Missing persons—Fiction. 4. Iceland—Fiction.] I. Title.
PZ7.S594Th 2010 [Fic]—dc22 2009018166

ISBN 978-0-375-86629-6 (tr. pbk.)

Printed in the United States of America

10 9 8 7 6 5 4 3 2 1

First Bluefire Edition 2011

Like Haley, I'm descended from a long line of strong
women. This one's for them: my grandmothers,
Anne Rosenel, Jenny Simner, and Isabel Simner;
my aunts, Harriet Piltz and Ida Rosenel;
and most of all my mother, Roberta Dunker,
the strongest woman I know
and the reason I grew up never doubting
I could be anything I wanted.

~ THIEF EYES ~

I will not allow it.

I will not be given to the first man who asks for my hand, bartered like a horse or a sheep. I will determine my fate, as my father promised me long ago.

My father's brother, Hrut, says none may determine their fate, not even Odin One-Eye and his kin. Hrut is a fool. He says I have the eyes of a thief and that men will suffer for me. He says it is the future he sees.

Let Hrut see what he will. I'll show him what a thief's eyes and thief's heart can truly do. I draw my scarlet cloak close. None can see me in this cave beyond the Law Rock. None can hear me over the water that roars beyond it.

I take a skin filled with a fox's blood and pour it into a wooden bowl—driftwood, come over waters I've never *sailed. I longed once to seek riches across the sea, and my father promised me that as well. Then he told me his promises were a child's game, nothing more. He told me I was no longer a child, and that my marriage to Thorvald, Osvif's son, was arranged.*

No matter. I have another uncle, Svan, a sorcerer who lives by Bear's Fjord to the north. Svan is my mother's brother, not my father's. When I asked him to teach me sorcery, he did not deem his promise a game.

I take a black raven's claw and pierce my thumb. Above the roar of the waterfall, a raven cries out, as if angered by the loss of its kin. What do ravens know of anger? I squeeze my thumb, using my own blood to draw a circle upon a dull black stone. A fire stone, cool in my hand, yet with heat enough to burn at its core. I cross the circle with three intersecting lines, then draw smaller lines and circles at their ends, combining the runes Svan taught me, one for possession, the other for time. The stone grows warm. I drop it into the fox's blood. I toss a smooth silver coin—no mark upon it—into the blood as well, and then I chant, shouting to hear myself over the water:

> *Powers beyond the earth, hear me!*
> *Powers beneath the earth, aid me!*
> *Find her, turn her,*
> *Show me her place!*

The blood begins to boil. I take a yellow ring, woven from strands of my own hair—a gift I gave my father long ago, meant to seal his promises. Those promises are broken. The ring is mine to give again where I will. I slip it over my finger and thrust my hand into the bowl.

The boiling blood burns, but I do not fear pain. My fingers close around the coin.

Flames leap up from the blood—the flames of another world, one of fiery giants and melting stone. The flames take on shapes as they roar all around me—a grasping hand, a gaping mouth. My skin blisters and melts away. Fire burns through my bare finger bones as the figures reach for my hands, my hair.

Then the flames fall away, and the cave walls with them. Through air that shimmers with heat I see a broad path beneath an open sky.

On that path, I see the years of my life laid out before me. I see beyond those years, to times when our warriors cast aside their swords and our weavers their looms, when our stories are turned to runes bound in leather, nothing more. Difficult times—but what time is not difficult? Better a difficult life than one controlled by others. So said my forebears when they parted ways with the Norwegian king and sailed for this land. So say I, as I look down the path.

I see my daughter, by Thorvald or another man, I cannot tell. She looks right at me—in this vision she is older *than I am—and nods sharply. She is angry, and not only at my spell. Crafted of my anger as the spell is, it is drawn to the anger in all my descendants' lives—to the moments of weakness when they might consent to my bargain.*

The air whispers of my daughter's anger—a slain son, caught unaware while sowing grain—but then she turns fiercely away. She is more interested in avenging this wrong than escaping it. I'm glad my spell won't land on her. I will go farther—beyond my life, and my daughter's life, and every last tie between my father and me.

I see my daughter's daughters, and their daughters in turn, the path they stand upon branching as it stretches through time. The air around each woman whispers of a different grief: a cruel husband, a slain lover, a hungry winter, a deadly fall of ash upon the fields. For thirty generations, every one of them meets my eyes—and turns away. My blood grows thin, but my daughters remain strong, too strong to flee these moments of pain.

The branches that do not bear daughters are lost to me, one by one, until only two branches of my descendants remain. On one, a woman with long red hair trembles beneath my gaze. I hear whispers of abandonment, of a man fled across the sea—it is often about a man. Yet she also turns away. She has no daughters, and so her branch, too, is lost.

The other branch slips out of my reach, its daughters growing ghostly and faint as they journey across a different sea—until one of them returns to this land, a woman with fair yellow hair like my own. She meets my gaze and doesn't turn away. I see the confusion upon her face: her line has forgotten much of magic. Tears streak her cheeks and make her gray eyes bright. The air around her whispers of betrayal, of a man lying in another woman's arms.

There is freedom in having a man leave you—but perhaps she does not know this. Perhaps she seeks escape after all.

I can give her that—and in so doing, seize the freedom for myself.

"A gift!" I call. The woman's eyes grow large as I draw the coin from the burning blood. There are symbols etched upon the silver now, the same signs I drew upon the stone. I throw the coin to her, through thirty generations of time. The woman hesitates, then reaches out a shaking hand and catches it.

The path trembles beneath us. A moment more and this woman and I will trade places. I will see through her eyes; she will see through mine. She will marry Thorvald, Osvif's son, and I will be free.

The woman looks away, as if startled—by my spell or by something else, I cannot tell. She blinks hard, drops the coin, and runs.

Foolish woman! You must never run from magic, least of all magic born of fire. Thirty generations is not time enough to forget that.

The fire returns, roaring around us both. The ground

lurches. *Flames leap at the woman. They burn through cloth and skin to ignite the bones beneath. She has no time to scream—in moments the fire consumes her.*

My sight clears. I kneel once more in this small cave, my hand yet immersed in boiling blood. I draw it free and overturn the bowl. Blood stains the dark rocks. My hand is whole and unburned, save for a band of red where the ring, woven of my own hair, used to be. The coin is gone, sent through thirty generations of time only to be dropped and lost in a single instant.

I touch the band of red and find it warm. I close my eyes. Flames roar up once more behind my lids. "Free!" an inhuman voice cries, somewhere deep inside me. A fiery hand strokes my face. "We will be free."

I know then that the spell is not through. The fire will consume me as well, and the powers that wield it will be released into the world. Yet through the flames, I see something more. One last daughter, with yellow hair and strange dark eyes. The fire's roar is loud; I cannot hear her whispered anger. She reaches for the coin where it fell into the dirt. The earth trembles once more as her fingers close around the silver.

The flames subside. The land grows still. I feel the power of the fire realm burning in me yet, but it is contained now within my hair—the same hair in my ring, the hair I gifted to the realm of fire—and also in the coin this new daughter now holds. My spell has been mended. My life has been spared.

Does this woman—no, this girl, for she is younger than I am—seek escape as well? I reach for her. She leans toward me, and I know the spell remains alive between us. Yet it is weaker now. The girl was not its target. I cannot simply take her place.

Not yet. Instead, I look at this daughter of my daughters and ask, "What is your name?"

～ Chapter 1 ～

Icy rain blew into my hood and dripped down my neck as I knelt on the mossy stones. The sky was gray, layers of cloud hiding any hint of sun. The wind picked up, and I shivered, missing the hot desert skies of home. It was way too cold for a June day.

Not that Dad noticed. He grinned as he traced a crack running through the rocks. "Amazing, isn't it? You can almost *feel* the earth pulling apart."

"Yeah. Sure." I looked down into the small fissure and saw nothing but endless dark. I shifted my soggy backpack on my shoulders and rubbed my eyes, gritty from a night spent flying across the Atlantic. I'd never been much good at sleeping on planes. *Yeah, Dad, I followed you four thousand miles to Iceland so we could stare at holes in the ground.*

I got up, stretching stiff legs. Beyond a metal fence, the cliff where we stood dropped down to a grassy plain. A gray river braided its way through bright green grasses, and a few wet geese hunkered down by its shores. The geese looked cold, too. Probably they were thinking the same thing I was: the sooner they could get somewhere warm, the better.

"So this is where it happened?" I tried to sound casual, like I didn't much care.

Dad looked up. His dark eyes were shot with red—he wasn't good at sleeping on planes, either—and his hair stuck out from beneath his windbreaker, dripping water. "You mean the rifting? It's happening throughout this valley. The North American and European tectonic plates meet here, and they're forever pulling away from each other. Only the pulling doesn't all happen in any one place, so—"

"That's not what I mean." I fought not to let my frustration show. *You know that's not what I mean.*

Dad sighed. "No, Haley, this isn't where it happened." His sleep-deprived eyes took on the lost look I'd come to know way too well this past year. The look that made me decide Dad didn't need to know if I'd blown another test at school, or fallen asleep in class because nightmares had woken me in the middle of the night again, or was tired of peanut butter and jelly for dinner but just as tired of cooking if I wanted anything else.

I'd come four thousand miles. This was more important than a few bad dreams or missed meals. "Where, then?"

A couple brushed past us, clutching the hands of the toddler who walked between them. Dad looked at the cracked earth. "*Logberg.* Law Rock."

"Where's that?" Rain soaked through my running shoes, turning my socks clammy and cold. Back home, we canceled track meets for weather like this—but I was the one who'd asked Dad to bring me here. He'd wanted to stay at the guesthouse and catch up on his jet-lagged sleep.

Dad sighed again. "You're not going to let this go, are you?"

Let this go? I dug my nails into my cold, damp palms. No need for Dad to hear me screaming, either. *When your mother disappears without a trace, you don't just let it go.* "I want to see. Is that so much to ask?" I kept my voice calm, reasonable—the same voice I'd used to convince Dad to take me to Thingvellir today, because I really wanted to visit the national park that was the site of Iceland's ancient parliament and in the middle of a rift valley and, oh, yeah, just happened to be the place where my mother disappeared last summer.

"Fine, Haley." Dad got to his feet, and I knew for once I'd won. I followed him away from the lookout, my running shoes squishing on the wet gravel path. Dripping tendrils escaped my blond ponytail and clung to my cheeks. I slowed to match Dad's pace. I'd grown taller than him this past year, which still seemed strange.

The path cut down through a cleft between blocky stone

walls that formed a perfect wind tunnel. Goose bumps prickled beneath my damp sleeves. Dad looked up at the rocks. "You can almost see how they must have fit together once, can't you? Before the rifting tugged them apart."

What I saw was my father hiding behind another geology lecture. Maybe Dad couldn't help it. Maybe when you spent your whole life studying rocks and earthquakes, you forgot how to talk to people.

The stone wall to our right dropped away as we reached a grassy outcrop. The wind let up, and Dad stopped at the base of a walkway that led to an overlook. Some tourists stood on the walkway, huddled beneath umbrellas, listening to a tour guide in jeans and a T-shirt. The guide was soaked, but he didn't seem to mind.

"Here?" I asked. Dad nodded.

Even without the wind, I felt cold. "So what'd you two fight about?" My voice came out too loud, with a squeak at the end. So much for sounding casual.

Dad leaned down, picked up a black stone, and turned it over in his hand. "Obsidian," he said. "It's funny how the names of rocks translate in Icelandic. Obsidian is literally raven flint, while lignite—brown coal—has something to do with the fire giants, out of Norse mythology—"

"Dad!"

He dropped the stone but didn't meet my eyes. "No, Haley."

"No what?"

"No, I'm not going to answer your question. Some things are none of your concern."

It's my concern more than anyone's! Dad never answered, no matter how often I asked. I dug my nails deeper into my palms, felt the familiar pinch of nails breaking skin. I whirled away and stomped up the wet walkway, past the tourists. Mom would have run after me, but Dad just let me go. I reached the overlook and leaned on a railing, staring out at the river. A goose made its way into the water, followed by two fuzzy goslings. I watched them sail by. There should have been squirrels here, too, chipmunks, *something*—but Iceland wasn't big on native land mammals. A few arctic foxes, the occasional stranded polar bear—that was it.

My palms began to sting. Behind me the guide talked cheerfully about all the old stories that were supposed to have happened at Thingvellir. Mostly they sounded like a long list of who killed who, though at least one guy managed to fall in love, get married, and take his wife east with him. That didn't sound so bad—except that years later, when he was battling enemies, his so-called true love refused her husband two locks of her long hair, which he needed to replace his severed bowstring. "Gunnar died, of course," the guide said.

Of course. The rain dripped down my hood and into my face. No happy endings *here*. No endings at all, just a polite

letter from Iceland's *Logreglan*—their police—concluding
that there was no sign of where my mother went but no ev-
idence of foul play, either. The story stopped there.

It stopped *here*. Mom had come to Iceland with Dad
last summer, the first summer of Dad's three-year research
grant. They'd visited Thingvellir to do some sightseeing,
and they'd gotten into a fight. Nothing strange about that—
Mom and Dad did fight sometimes. Whose parents don't?
Well, okay, my boyfriend Jared's, but that was beside the
point. They were mostly stupid fights, anyway, about stuff
like Dad spending too much time on campus, or Mom
bringing home yet another stray cat to foster, or whose turn
it was to cook or pay the bills.

As I stared out at the river, I could almost picture them
here: Mom in her slacks and blouse, blond hair loose
around her shoulders—she only pulled it back for work at
her vet clinic; Dad in his rumpled T-shirt and jeans, his
mad-scientist hair sticking out in all directions. Mom would
do all the yelling, of course. Dad got really quiet when they
fought. But then it would be over and life would go on. Except this time, Mom had been so mad that instead of making up with Dad like she was supposed to, she'd run away.
Dad had waited for Mom to cool down and come back.
She never did.

Dad had let me read the police report, but he wouldn't
tell me what he and Mom had fought about. So I gave up

asking and started begging him to take me to Iceland with him instead. I'd figured once we were here he'd *have* to explain.

So much for that theory. I stared at the wet wooden slats beneath my feet. What could make Mom so angry she'd decide not to come home? How well could she hide in a country smaller than Arizona? How could she want to, when I was home waiting for her? Did she hate me as much as she hated Dad? Mom and I fought, too, also about stupid things, like whether I'd washed the dishes or could cut my hair or was old enough to date. Mom wouldn't abandon me for any of *that* . . . would she?

The wind picked up again, cutting right through my fleece-lined jacket. What if something else had happened, like some creepy kidnapper or human trafficker had spirited Mom away? Was she even still alive? My stomach clenched at the thought, even as I told myself that of course Mom was okay. We'd know if something really awful had happened to her—wouldn't we?

If Dad knew anything—anything at all—he had to tell me. I'd *make* him tell me. I turned from the railing and headed back to him.

At the end of the walkway I stopped short. Someone was staring at Dad, a woman in a long wool skirt and deep green jacket. Her hood was pulled back in spite of the rain, her flyaway hair barely tamed in a long red braid. Dad drew his arms around himself, as if he'd only just noticed the weather. "Katrin. We're not meeting until tomorrow."

Wait, that was Katrin Jonsdottir? Dad's coauthor—they'd written a bunch of papers together about new ways to predict earthquakes and volcanoes.

"Umm, hi," I said, then realized I'd spoken in English. *"Godan daginn,"* I tried instead, words from the Icelandic phrase book I'd read on the plane.

Katrin frowned. The wind blew damp strands into her face. "You must be Haley." Her English was perfect, just the slightest trace of an accent. She gave Dad a look cold enough to freeze water, and I wondered how they even sat in the same room together, let alone wrote all those papers. "You shouldn't have brought her here," Katrin said.

"Excuse me?" *Nice to meet you, too.* Maybe Katrin was one of those people who hated all teenagers on general principle—but no, Dad had said she had a kid, too.

Dad shrugged uneasily. "Haley and I don't mind the rain."

"I'm not talking about the rain," Katrin said. The look that passed between her and Dad should have turned that rain to jagged shards of ice.

"Haley, why don't you go on ahead?" Dad said. "I'll catch up."

"Sure, Dad." I didn't want to watch him and Katrin stare at each other a moment more. If I did, I thought I might turn to ice, too. What was going on here? And why did the stomach-clenching feeling I had—the same feeling I got when Mom and Dad fought—tell me I didn't want to know?

Before I could make a break for it, Katrin laid a hand on my shoulder. I was afraid she'd tell me to stay, but she said only, "Be careful, Haley," before looking back to Dad.

"Umm, yeah. Okay." I turned away from her and hurried down the path. After a few steps I broke into a jog, ignoring the way my sneakers squelched against the gravel. Running felt good after seventeen hours waiting in airports and being crammed into airplane seats meant for short people. For the first time since landing in Iceland, I almost felt warm.

The path led to a pond with an interpretive sign. I stopped to read it, stretching my calves and watching raindrops ripple the water's surface. The sign explained that in the Middle Ages, women convicted of things like lying and adultery had been drowned here. *Nice.*

A bit of sun fought its way through the clouds, making the water seem red, like blood. I shivered and ran on, following a dirt trail that branched away from the main path, winding around the far side of the pond and then following a stream uphill.

The rain slowed to a few soggy drips. The path grew steeper and water roared in the distance. *Be careful.* I scowled, remembering Katrin's warning. Careful of what? I kept climbing. A huge waterfall came into view.

Huge if you lived in southern Arizona, anyway. White spray leaped into the air. I left the path and clambered over slippery rocks, trying to get closer to the water. The roaring grew louder, the air colder. Too cold—I stopped and rubbed the sleeves of my wet jacket. What was I doing here, anyway? What made me think I could find Mom, when the people who actually lived here had failed?

Spray blew into my face. A few more threads of sun poked through the clouds, casting rainbow patterns onto the water. *Beautiful,* I thought, but I only felt colder. I wondered if Mom had seen this same waterfall. "Where *is* she?" I asked the rushing water. Of course it didn't answer. I sighed, turned around, and clambered back down to the trail.

Something glinted in the dirt there. A small silver coin, not much bigger than my thumbnail, crisscrossed with a strange pattern of circles and lines. I knelt down, as somewhere a raven cried out, and picked the thing up.

The coin burned as my fingers closed around it. The ground shook as if a train were going by. The air blurred and a hot desert wind stroked my cheek. I should have been scared, but that heat felt so good after the chill rain. I clutched the coin harder and leaned into the wind. The roaring waterfall seemed very far away.

Somewhere a woman's voice whispered, *"Hvad heitir thu?"*

I knew that from my phrase book, too. I frowned, trying to remember the right response. *"Eg heiti Haley."*

Someone touched my shoulder. The air snapped back into focus, and rain spattered from the cold sky onto the trail. I turned around, looking for the woman who'd asked my name. No one stood there but Dad. "Ready to go?" He shouted to be heard over the water.

I shoved the coin into my pocket. It felt merely warm now, like it had been too long in the sun. Maybe I was just homesick and had imagined the desert wind. But why would I have imagined a woman's voice to go with it?

I followed Dad back down the trail. "Did you feel the earthquake?" he asked, once the waterfall was far enough away that he didn't have to shout.

"Earthquake?" I remembered the ground shaking— was that what an earthquake felt like? Did the air usually go all blurry during a quake?

"Just a small one." Dad grinned, like he couldn't wait for the ground to rattle and shake some more. "Earthquakes, volcanoes—really, Iceland's just one huge geologic event waiting to happen."

Now there's a comforting thought. I stepped past the drowning pool and onto the main gravel path.

Katrin ran up to us, her braid flying out behind her, and looked right at me. "You're okay?" The anger was gone, and her face was pinched with worry.

"I'm fine." Was there some reason I shouldn't be? "It was just a small quake." I smiled, but Katrin didn't smile back.

She looked sharply at Dad. "Tomorrow, Gabe. Both of you."

Dad sighed, as if he found the idea troubling. "Yes, Katrin. We'll be there."

Katrin nodded and walked away without another word. I looked at Dad.

"Lunch," he said. "We're meeting to talk about this summer's observation stations, and Katrin invited you along." Dad shoved his hood back and ran a hand through his unruly hair. Before I could ask why Katrin would want me to come to lunch when she thought I shouldn't be here at all, he said, "Speaking of food, what do you say we get some dinner?" Dad blinked hard, like he did when he stayed up too late working on a paper.

I rubbed my eyes, too. A night without sleep was enough to make the world seem more than a little blurry, right? "Dinner sounds good."

"We'll get hot dogs," Dad said. "Iceland has the best lamb hot dogs—"

"Yeah, Dad." I laughed. "I came four thousand miles just to eat hot dogs."

Dad laughed, too, and for a moment the tiredness left his face. It wasn't only the flight—he'd looked more tired at home, too, since Mom had disappeared. I knew how he felt.

I *had* to find her. For both of us. I'd have dinner first, and try to get some sleep—and then I'd make Dad answer my questions. Or else I'd go look for Mom on my own. No way was I letting this go. I followed Dad back to the car. My hand itched, and I glanced down at it.

There was a small red circle on my palm, right over the red half-moons where I'd dug my nails in—right where the coin had burned me.

~∿·Chapter 2 ᴄ~

The red mark had long faded by the time we ate dinner and returned to our guesthouse in Reykjavik. It was nearly ten by then, not that you could tell by the sun, which was low but still up, shining like an old quarter through layers of gray. I scribbled a postcard to Jared, changed into an oversized T-shirt, and crawled into bed. I was so, so tired. I clutched Mortimer, the stuffed brown wombat no one but Mom knew I slept with, and let soft sleep wrap around me, hoping for once I'd sleep without dreams.

Yeah right. Just because I'd traveled thousands of miles and not slept for two days, what made me think the universe would give me a break?

I dreamed of a gray tower of toy blocks, stacked on a golden hillside. Dandelions had rooted in the blocks and

gone to seed. Little white-and-black birds perched on their
heights.*

*I dreamed of a bow made of fire. Someone drew the
bowstring back, and a burning arrow arced through the
air. The arrow struck the hillside; the ground shuddered
and gaped open where it fell. More flames leaped up from
beneath the earth. Birds screamed and fled. Blocks caught
fire as they tumbled to the ground.*

*The flames leaped higher, turning into grasping arms
that were made, like the bow, all of fire. I ran, and as I did
I felt something catch beneath my skin. I knew then the fire
was in me, not the earth, after all.*

*The acrid stench of smoke filled the air. "You must
never run from sorcery," a voice yelled, but I just ran faster,
struggling to breathe through the smoke, while my skin
melted away and my bones crumbled to ash—*

I bolted upright in bed, sweat pouring down my face.
Something burned in my hand—I opened my eyes and saw
the small silver coin, engraved with its pattern of circles and
lines. I flung the thing across the room. I'd left it in my jeans
last night. I knew I had.

I sat there, gasping for breath, trying to shake off the
nightmare. Sweat plastered my T-shirt to my skin. "Just a
dream," I whispered. Slowly, the fear that burned through
me faded. I had nightmares all the time now. Usually they
were about Mom: Mom being kidnapped, Mom falling into
a ravine, Mom being stabbed or shot or simply getting lost

and calling my name. By day I told myself Mom had to be all right, but at night I dreamed about every possible awful thing that could have happened to her.

Mom hadn't been in this dream, but I still had that stomach-aching, hands-trembling, after-nightmare feeling. "Just a dream." I kept whispering so I wouldn't wake Dad. Dad never knew what to do when I had nightmares; he just looked lost. I needed Mom here, to stroke my hair and chase the dreams away.

At least it was morning. Sun shone around the drawn shades. Through the thin wall I heard Dad talking about pyroclastic flows in his sleep. I dug Mortimer out from beneath the covers and hugged him close. The old wombat's eyes had fallen out long ago and had been replaced with mismatched buttons. The thread of his seams was a different color each place Mom had patched him up. Mom was always bringing me stuffed animals, every one a different species and none of them the standard bear. Still holding Mortimer, I leaned back and shut my eyes.

Flames danced behind my eyelids. I leaped to my feet, breathing hard. "Just a dream," I said, over and over. "Just a stupid dream." My hands shook, and I tasted ash at the back of my throat. No way was I closing my eyes again.

I dug through my suitcase instead, pulled out running pants and a tank top, and got dressed for a run. My track coach was impressed by how much I'd practiced this past year, picking up county honors as a sophomore. I didn't tell him I didn't run for the honors. I ran because running chased the nightmares away.

My hands trembled as I laced up my sneakers. I glanced at the clock—4:17, it read. I groaned. It wasn't morning. It was just Iceland, where the sun barely set in summer and barely rose in winter. I wasn't about to go back to sleep, though. I pulled my tangled hair into a ponytail, wrote a note for Dad and taped it to the fridge, and headed out. The clouds and the rain were gone, leaving behind a deep blue sky and low pale sun. The cool air smelled heavy with water. It felt good against my sweaty skin.

My trembling eased as I headed down the gray brick sidewalk at a brisk pace, warming cold muscles. *Just a dream.* Concrete buildings lined the street, painted red and blue and green, like toy houses. A woman pushed a stroller toward me. The baby inside slept quietly. The woman's eyes were red, as if she hadn't slept nearly as well. I smiled in sympathy, but she didn't smile back.

I broke into a slow jog. The dream faded, the memory of flames turning less real than the slap of my rubber soles on the pavement and the music blaring from a distant bar. Bright blue water shone in the distance. I headed toward it. Somewhere a car horn honked—a quiet honk, oddly polite. Two small white birds with red beaks, black caps, and long tail feathers stared at me from a rooftop. Arctic terns? Somewhere farther away, a raven krawked, and the little birds flew off abruptly. I was less interested in birds than in mammals, but I remembered that arctic terns migrated all the way from the Arctic to Antarctica and back again, every single year. They were tough little birds.

The street met a paved black trail that followed the bay, beside a seawall built of large gray rocks. Perfect—I turned right, onto the path, and broke into a faster run. Sun reflected off the water beside me. Across the bay, smooth black volcanic hills swept toward the sky, so different from the dusty brown mountains of home. Different, but kind of cool—I stared at them as I ran. In the distance I heard barking.

Something furry barreled into my legs. I tumbled to the pavement, speed turning to stillness in an instant. A wet tongue licked my face.

Someone pulled the dog away and began speaking—angry Icelandic words I didn't understand. It was a boy around my age, with a wool cap jammed down over his ears and shaggy brown hair that fell into his eyes. He knelt in front of me, his arms overflowing with a wriggling brown-and-white Icelandic sheepdog.

"I'm sorry, I don't—*Talar thu ensku?*" I asked hopefully. That was on the very first page of my phrase book.

The boy's mouth pulled into a sardonic smile. He wore a scuffed black leather jacket, mended at the elbows. "Yes, of course I speak English. I yell at the dog, not you. Though you do not look like a tourist."

I laughed. "I'll take that as a compliment." My great-great-grandmother had come from Iceland, but that hardly

seemed to count. I got to my feet. My running pants were
torn, and the scraped skin beneath bled from a jagged gash.
I flexed my knee and felt a twinge of pain.

The boy glanced at the scrape. "Sorry," he said. The
dog squirmed out of his arms and licked my knee, making
the rip larger. His rough tongue stung, but I didn't flinch
away. I drew the dog into a hug, rubbing his shaggy fur and
letting him know I forgave him for knocking me over. He
licked my face, as if he forgave me, too, for not watching
where I was going.

"He likes you." The boy stood and offered me his handkerchief. He was taller than he seemed—taller than me.
"Are you okay?"

"I'm fine." I took the handkerchief—he had lovely long
fingers—and did my best to wipe the blood away. I stood,
testing the weight on my knee. Already the pain was fading
and the bleeding slowing. I reached down to scratch the
dog behind the ears. He was a sweet dog, with one of those
always-questioning faces. "What's his name?"

"Flosi," the boy said.

I rubbed Flosi's nose. Flosi nudged my hand away, gave
my knee an enthusiastic final lick—that stung, too—and
looked up at the boy.

"We need to go," the boy said.

"Yeah." Of course he had to go. No reason for him to
hang around chatting with some random tourist his dog

had toppled over. Still, we both hesitated. In the sunlight, his green eyes were nearly as bright as the sea.

We looked away at the same instant. My face felt hot. There was no reason for that, either.

"Sorry," the boy said again.

"No harm done." I smiled. Then, because I didn't want him to think *I* was the one hanging around too long, I added a "see you" and jogged off. My knee hurt at first, but I'd run through worse, and the pain disappeared as I found my pace once more. I realized I still held the boy's handkerchief, but when I glanced back, he was already gone. I shoved it into my pocket, thinking about the way his shaggy brown hair fell into his face, over those bright eyes.

There was definitely no reason to be thinking about his eyes. I turned my thoughts to Jared, in his jeans and the sleeveless T-shirts he wore even in winter, his arms well muscled from hours spent helping with his family's landscaping business. Jared's hair was clipped close to his neck and never fell into his face. We'd only started dating this past year, but we'd been friends forever. I needed to find a net café to e-mail him—my cell phone didn't work in Iceland, and it felt strange being out of touch. Jared was doing a wildlife biology internship in San Diego this summer. Before I'd decided to go to Iceland, I was supposed to intern there with him. Jared and I both wanted to work with animals one day, not in a clinic but in the wild.

I ran past houses and apartment buildings, offices and warehouses. Sweat trickled down my neck and into my eyes. A few cars drove past on the nearby road. A duck with brown feathers and a bright green head drifted by on the water. Given how little Dad was willing to tell me, maybe I should have gone to San Diego. I felt a twinge of anger at the thought.

A warm wind picked up. A desert wind—it dried the sweat and caressed my arms, just like at home. The air shimmered, as if with heat haze.

"Haley," a voice whispered. That voice tugged on some thread anchored deep inside me. I skidded to a halt.

A woman in a long scarlet cloak stood atop the seawall. She was just a few years older than me, her eyes a smoldering gray, her blond hair so long it blew about her calves. I should have seen blue sky behind her, but instead I saw black stone. I caught the faint scent of hot ash. *"Haley."*

It was the same voice I'd heard at Thingvellir. She reached out a hand, and the gesture pulled at me, too. I stepped toward her, not sure why, not sure whether I had a choice. My feet clambered up onto the seawall. The ground trembled. "Who are you?" My voice shook, which surprised me.

The woman spoke sharp Icelandic words I couldn't understand—a question? Her accent was very different than the boy's had been. She reached for my hand, and her fingers slid, ghostlike, right through mine. A wave of dizziness washed over me. The hot wind blew on. I swayed and reached for the woman in turn, not sure if I was awake or asleep.

A raven's cry cut the air. A gust of cold wind blew. I stumbled and fell from the seawall, into the icy water. Rocks jabbed my arms and cut through my running pants. The woman cried out in anger. More faintly, I heard beating wings.

I staggered to my feet, dripping water, the sea up past my knees. The blue sky was gone; I could barely make out the fog-shrouded seawall above me. That made no sense. How could fog move in so fast? It raised goose bumps on my arms, which were covered with gritty black sand. I climbed back up onto the seawall.

The woman had vanished. That didn't make sense, either. For a moment the wings beat on. Then another gust of wind blew, and I knew only that I was too, too cold.

I stumbled back down to the paved path I'd run on, teeth beginning to chatter. Wet, itchy sand had gotten down beneath my tank top. My skin felt like ice, and the fog was like ice, too. Only my hand was still warm, my fingers clenched around some small hot coal. I unclenched them and saw the silver coin. I swore and flung it into the sea, then immediately missed its warmth.

I shivered violently, barely noticing the small red circle on my palm again. God, I was cold. The buildings had disappeared into the fog, but I could still see the seawall and the paved running trail. I ran back toward the guesthouse, hoping that running would warm me up. There were rocks in my squelching shoes. I didn't care. I ran faster, desperate for any warmth I could find.

The fog slowly cleared. The sun was always so low here—I couldn't tell what time it was. My knee had stopped bleeding, and the sea had washed the blood away. Instead of the jagged gash that had been there, I saw only an angry red scab.

As if I'd been running for quite some time.

❦ *Chapter 3* ❧

Ｂy the time I reached the guesthouse, the fog had cleared and my knee ached again. My lips were numb, and so were the tips of my fingers and toes. I threw the door open and stumbled into the entryway, soaking in the wonderful indoor warmth.

It took me a moment to realize that Dad stood there, watching me. He wore jeans and yesterday's shirt, and his hair stuck out in even more directions than usual. He trembled as he grabbed me into a hug. "Haley, where were you?"

I drew back and looked at him. "Just out for a run. I left a note."

Dad shook his head. "That was *six hours ago*."

What? "No, I only ran a few miles, I—"

Dad turned his watch to me—10:30, it read. "I've been

out looking for you." His voice was tight, like a string about to snap. "I was getting ready to call the police."

My wet clothes felt clammy and cold. "That's impossible." No way had I been running for six hours. I thought of the sudden fog; that should have been impossible, too. Was I going insane? If Dad couldn't handle a few nightmares, what would he do if I lost it completely?

I stretched my cooling calves, not looking at him. "Guess I'm still learning my way around." I tried to keep my voice light—a nothing-to-worry-about-here voice. "Took a few wrong turns. Sorry."

Dad reached out and touched my damp hair. It had fallen out of its elastic and hung limp about my face. He glanced at my torn pants. "Haley, is there something I should know?"

"Oh, yeah." I forced a laugh. "Some boy's dog ran into me, tripped me up pretty good." I pulled off my sodden shoes and set them on the shoe rack by the door.

"You ran." Dad's voice was little more than a whisper.

"I'm a runner, of course I—" The words stuck in my throat as I realized what he meant. "No, not like that!" I hadn't run *away,* not like Mom. I rubbed at my damp arms. A rock inside one of my soaked socks dug into my toe. "I told you, I got lost!"

"I know what you told me." Dad's face set into firmer lines. "But I'm telling you something, too, Haley. I won't leave Iceland without you. Do you understand that?"

My fingertips and lips were still cold. I wanted to get out of there, into a warm shower. "I said I was sorry."

"Do you understand?"

"I lost track of the time, I—" I couldn't meet Dad's steady gaze. How could he even think I'd run away? "I understand," I muttered.

"Good," Dad said. I couldn't tell whether he believed me or not. "Go get changed, then, or we'll be late for lunch."

I bolted for my room, leaving wet footprints on the wooden floor. I had a sudden fierce thought: *How come you left without Mom?* I grabbed shampoo and a towel and headed for the shower. I knew well enough why Dad had left Iceland last summer—to look after me. But I could have stayed with Grandma in Yuma a few weeks longer, or else with Jared's family back in Tucson when school started. Why had *Dad* let this go?

I peeled off my wet clothes—it felt good to get out of them—and turned on the shower. Warm water burned against my skin, chasing the last of my shivers away. The water held a faint rotten-egg sulfur smell. I thought of the woman on the seawall, of the hot ash scent before I fell into the bay. I turned the water up. Steam rose around me, and the numbness left my fingers and toes. I knew well enough that the smell came from the geothermal vents that heated the whole city. Hot water by volcano, Dad had said.

Fire leaping up from beneath the earth—I scrubbed

fiercely at my scraped knee, only stopping when the scab began to bleed. I didn't want to think about my dreams, any more than I wanted to think about the long-haired woman and the way her hand had gone right through mine. I glanced down at my own hands. The red circle from the coin was gone—again. I saw only half-moon scabs that were already healing. The pale white scars beneath them seemed to have settled in for good this past year, though.

Steam fogged the shower door. What if I really was going insane?

Could Mom have gone crazy, too? Crazy enough to dream of fire and see ghosts and fall into the sea? Was *that* what Dad didn't want to tell me?

I drew a shuddering breath and coughed on sulfur-scented steam. This wasn't just about some nightmares or a few failed tests. Whatever was going on, I should talk to Dad. If he couldn't cope, maybe he'd find someone who could. Maybe this was a matter for professionals.

It'd be easier to talk to Mom. I want to talk to Mom. I turned off the water and watched the steam disappear. *Tomorrow,* I promised myself. I'd get some sleep, make sure I didn't just have the worst case of jet lag ever, and then I'd talk to Dad.

I wrapped myself in the towel, dug some Band-Aids out of the first-aid kit Dad had stuck in the medicine cabinet, and ducked into my room. As I pulled on jeans and a Desert Museum T-shirt, I heard Dad start the shower.

I still had the boy's bloody handkerchief. Meeting him and Flosi, at least, had been real. I shoved the handkerchief into my jeans pocket, a reminder that I wasn't crazy about *everything*. I ran a brush through my wet hair and pulled it up into a new elastic. Then I jammed a water bottle and the phrase book into my backpack, grabbed my jacket, and headed into the kitchen. I felt a little better after the shower. I filled a bowl with cornflakes and poured on the milk.

Or what I thought was milk—I sputtered and only barely managed to swallow. When we'd gone shopping on the way home last night, my phrase book had insisted *mjolk* was milk—but this tasted like yogurt mixed with sour cream. I dumped in a bunch of the Noa Kropp malt balls I'd also bought. They didn't taste like malt balls, either—more like chocolate-covered Rice Krispies—but at least they helped take the edge off. I stashed the rest of the bag in my backpack, in case lunch was no better than breakfast.

Dad joined me in the kitchen as I spooned up the last few bits of chocolate. Mom wouldn't have approved of mixing candy with breakfast. Dad didn't even notice. He was dressed up, for Dad, in khakis and a button-down shirt, his hair combed into submission. I tossed the bowl into the sink and we headed out.

The sun was bright, the sky so blue I wondered if I hadn't imagined the fog after all. Dad focused on the road and on shifting gears in our small rental car, but he kept stealing glances at me, like he wanted to ask what had really happened during those six hours. I stared out the window, where a few puffy white clouds clung to a black volcanic hillside. No, not clouds—steam, rising up from within the earth, like a mini-volcano. At the base of the hill a green field was streaked with bright yellow dandelions. Didn't they know better than to grow in a place like that, where molten fire could wipe them out at any time? We drove past more black hills and more stretches of startling green, dotted with purple and yellow wildflowers. In a field, a pair of shaggy-maned Icelandic horses scratched each other's backs with their blocky teeth as we drove past.

Silence stretched between Dad and me. The green gave way to a rocky gray wilderness, the rocks to a grassy hillside with a shining blue lake down below. Beyond the lake I saw the gray walls of the rift valley, row upon row of them. Dad turned, turned again, and pulled into a parking lot beneath the cliff we'd stood on yesterday, in front of a red-and-white building a road sign had labeled the Hotel Valholl.

Cold wind hit me as I got out of the car, in spite of the clear sky. "It really didn't feel like six hours," I told Dad.

He sighed and ran a hand through his hair—so much for his combing it—and I knew he didn't believe me. I sighed, too, and followed him inside, past an entryway hung with—yuck!—animal skins, and into a small dining room. A gray-haired couple in matching puffin sweatshirts sat at one table, a boy scribbling in a notebook at another. The boy closed the notebook and looked up. I blinked hard. It was Flosi's owner.

His hat was still jammed over his ears, but he'd hung his leather jacket over his chair, revealing a faded *Star Wars* T-shirt. His mouth quirked into a smile. "You're Haley, then?" As I wondered how he knew, Dad crossed the room to shake his hand. "You've grown, Ari."

"That is the usual way of things." His smile stiffened as he shook Dad's hand. He quickly turned to me as I walked up beside Dad. "So you see, I have a name as well."

My face grew hot. I realized I'd asked his dog's name but not his.

"Mom went to get some things from the car," Ari continued, still not looking at Dad. "She'll be right back."

"Wait—you're Katrin's son?"

"So they tell me," he said dryly. He had more of an accent than his mother did.

Dad took the seat across from Ari. I sat down next to Dad and draped my jacket over the back of my chair. "It's nice that you could join us," Dad said.

"Yeah, well, I never turn down food. I invited myself, actually." Ari stared at me through those green eyes, like he was trying to figure something out. "Flosi forgives you, by the way. The women do like to throw themselves at him. It is a problem."

My face flushed hotter. Was he *flirting* with me? How did you say "no, sorry, I have a boyfriend" in Icelandic? Or in English, for that matter? It wasn't like it had ever come up before.

Dad cleared his throat, and I realized I'd been staring back at Ari. I looked quickly down. "We met on my run," I said.

"Would that be before you got lost or afterward?" Dad's voice grew quiet.

"Before," I said.

"She tried to kill my dog," Ari agreed cheerfully.

"Well, Flosi does have a way of getting underfoot." Dad laughed, but there was an uneasy edge to it. "So that's how you tore your pants?"

"Yeah."

"And is it also how your clothes got wet?"

"Well, no, but—" I fell silent as Katrin slid into the chair beside Ari and dumped a pile of geology books onto the table.

"Hello, Katrin," Dad said.

Katrin didn't answer him. She looked right at me. There were tired circles around her eyes. "I don't suppose there's any chance you'd take the next plane back to the States?"

Right. Katrin really did want to get rid of me, though I had no idea why. I shook my head firmly. "Not unless you plan to put my mom and dad *both* on that plane home."

Dad flinched, but Ari looked up with interest. Of course—his mom probably knew what had happened, and she'd probably told him. At least he didn't look like he felt sorry for me, the way some of my friends at school had.

"Very well. If you insist on staying, there are some things you need to know." Katrin's expression turned businesslike. She handed me a small yellow spiral notebook from the pile, like one of Dad's waterproof field notebooks. "For you, Haley. Had you grown up here, you'd have had a copy years ago, but there's no helping that now."

I flipped through the pages. They were filled with a mix of cramped writing and strange symbols—squiggles and circles and lines. The waterproof paper felt slippery against my fingers.

"Read it through," Katrin said. "Let me know if you have any questions. Your mother—"

I pressed the notebook shut. "What do you know about my mother?"

Katrin drew a long breath. "There is no easy way to say this. Your mother got caught by a sorcerer's spell."

I stared at her, not sure I'd heard right. Dad set his hands down on the table. "Not this again," he said in his quiet angry voice.

Katrin's fierce gray eyes reminded me of the woman on the seawall. "Yes, this again, Gabe, and perhaps now you'll listen."

I was listening. I shoved the notebook into my pack.

Magic seemed as good an explanation for this morning as anything else. "There was this woman, I saw her on my run—" I stopped, realizing how stupid I sounded. If I mentioned my missing six hours, I'd sound stupider still.

"You didn't mention any woman before," Dad said.

"With long hair," Katrin said. Her face pinched into the same worried look as yesterday. "In a red cloak."

"How—who *is* she?"

"Who is *who*?" Dad demanded. Ari looked back and forth between us, opened his mouth as if to say something, and closed it again. A waiter walked up, left menus at the edge of the table, and quickly departed. Ari grabbed one and disappeared behind it.

Katrin laced her hands together. "*Hallgerdur Hoskuldsdottir*—Hallgerd, you'd say in English. Hallgerd was— some say she was a spoiled child who didn't get her way. Others say she was just a woman seeking a way out of an unwanted marriage. A thousand years ago, Hallgerd's father betrothed her to a man she didn't care for. Everyone knows this story—it's in our sagas. Only the sagas don't tell that Hallgerd was a sorcerer, and that she cast a spell to get out of her first marriage. She meant to find someone—some descendant of hers—to change places with. In doing so she hoped to escape to another time."

"And leave someone else stuck with the guy instead?" I asked. *What does this have to do with me? Why am I seeing this woman?*

"Hallgerd called on power deep within the earth for her spell," Katrin said. "That power echoes on to the present day, in the patterns of the plates that shift beneath our feet and the fires that stir the earth."

Dad rolled his eyes. "Or the plates could be shifting because Iceland is located both atop a hot spot and on the Mid-Atlantic Ridge, making it one of the most geologically active places on the entire planet."

"The spell failed," Katrin said, as if she hadn't heard, "so Hallgerd sent her—her foster father, that's the best translation, though it's not quite right—to kill her husband Thorvald instead, after Thorvald slapped her during a fight. Her foster father killed her second husband, too, though it's less clear Hallgerd wanted that. As for Hallgerd's third husband—he died when she refused him her hair to make a new string for his bow."

Gunnar died, of course. I remembered the tour guide saying that. How much did you have to hate someone to refuse him a few strands of your hair?

"She was quite the charmer," Ari said from behind his menu.

Katrin glanced at Ari, then back at me. "But all of that was later," she said. "First Hallgerd cast the spell on her descendants—on her daughter and her daughter's daughters, all the way down the line. Not many of her descendants remain, but I'm one, and your mother was another, only I didn't know that when she came here."

"Wait—we're related?" *And Dad just happened to wind up working with Mom's long-lost cousin?*

Ari snorted. "No more related than most Icelanders," he said. "This is not a large island, Haley. I'm more closely related to the prime minister than to you."

"The common ancestor was some twenty generations back," Katrin said. "You're probably more closely related to your president, too. And we probably have other common ancestors closer than Hallgerd—but that is not the point. The point is that Hallgerd searched for one of us to possess. For thirty generations, we all knew to turn away from her spell. Until your mother—" A pained look crossed Katrin's face. "She probably didn't even understand what Hallgerd offered her."

Dad shoved his menu aside. "We don't have to listen to this."

I ignored him. "What happened to Mom?"

Katrin swallowed and looked down at her laced fingers. "I'm so sorry. I didn't know Amanda was one of Hallgerd's daughters—that she was part of the line that had left for North America—until it was too late. I would have warned her, but—she ran, and so the spell consumed her."

"Consumed?" My throat tightened around the word.

Dad grabbed my hand. "I won't have you upsetting Haley with this nonsense."

Katrin glared at him. "Better for her to be upset and alive. What you need to know, Haley, is that you're one of

Hallgerd's daughters, too. And while the spell should have ended with your mother, it hasn't. I don't understand why, but the power Hallgerd called upon is with us still. You felt the earthquake yesterday. I think the problem may be— there's a coin that Hallgerd used to cast her spell. And that coin hasn't been found."

My hand fell limp in Dad's hold. My stomach did a little flip.

"It's possible," Katrin said, "that the coin was consumed as well, but—"

"No. It wasn't." I drew my hand free and reached into my pocket. I was only a little surprised to feel warm metal there. Sweat trickled down my neck. I'd thrown the coin away—in my room, and by the water, too. Somehow it always found me again.

I pulled it out and set it on the table. The symbol on it looked a little like the symbols in Katrin's notebook.

Katrin's shoulders stiffened. She grabbed my hands, not noticing the scars there. "You're unharmed?"

I nodded, frightened by her intense gaze, feeling a headache starting up. I forced myself to focus on Katrin's words.

"The coin must be returned to Hallgerd, at Hlidarendi in the east, where she used to live," Katrin said. "Thorgerd— that's Hallgerd's daughter—left instructions for her descendants, and they were very clear on this point. Perhaps the spell will not be done until we follow those instructions.

There've been too many small quakes this past year, and the pattern they form is unsettling. Yet if we return the coin, maybe the pattern will be ended."

"Enough." Dad's chair scraped the floor as he shoved it back. "Amanda *ran away*." Did I think his voice was quiet before? It had been loud compared to how softly he spoke now. "We fought, and she ran, and no one knows what happened next. I'll regret that fight—and other things, too, Katrin—for the rest of my life, but there was *no magic involved*."

I stared at the coin, afraid it would find its way back into my pocket if I dared look away. Katrin picked it up, then dropped it as if burned. The coin clattered to the table. "You'll have to carry it," she said, frowning. "We should go now. I don't know how much time we have, but I'll do what I can to save you from your mother's fate."

"Bullshit." Ari threw his menu down. He looked *furious*. "You use magic as an excuse for everything. Tell Haley what really happened." He glanced at Dad, then back to his mom. "Tell her the real reason neither of you followed Amanda when she ran."

I looked at Katrin. "Wait—you were there?"

"That's enough, Ari," Dad said.

"It is not enough!" Ari said. "I cannot *believe* you did not tell her."

"Tell me what?" The stomach-clenching, I-don't-want-to-know feeling returned, stronger than yesterday.

Katrin said something to Ari in Icelandic. It sounded like a warning.

Ari answered her in English. "Yes, well, if you and Gabe had kept your hands off of each other, maybe Amanda would not have run."

"*What?*"

Dad let out a breath and sank down into his seat. Katrin said something sharp in Icelandic and pointed to the door.

Ari answered her in Icelandic this time, his scorn clear enough. "I am sorry, Haley," he said to me in English. "But it is not sorcery I am sorry for." He grabbed his leather jacket and notebook and stalked out.

I looked from Katrin to Dad. My chest felt tight. "Is it—" The words stuck in my throat. "Did you—"

Dad shut his eyes. He looked utterly, completely lost.

The room felt too hot, too close. I didn't *care* how lost Dad felt, not if he—but he couldn't have—he wouldn't have. I stood, grabbing my own jacket and backpack as I did.

"Haley," Katrin said. "Until the coin is returned, you remain in danger. Hallgerd's spell could consume you yet."

"You—" I couldn't get enough air. I couldn't stand to even *look* at her. Had she and Dad really— I whirled away and bolted down the hall, pulling on my jacket as I did.

"Haley!" Katrin shouted, right across the restaurant. "You must *never* run from magic!"

I burst out the door and across the hotel parking lot.

Sun shone off the asphalt as I ran, pack bumping against my shoulders. Katrin ran after me, Dad close behind. I didn't slow down. If I ran, I didn't have to think—about Mom, about magic, about Dad and Katrin. My sneakers crunched as I turned onto a gray gravel path. The gravel gave way to dirt, and gray geese flew up from the river to my right. Ahead of me I saw the blocky walls of the rift valley outlined against a bright blue sky. Dad and Katrin both shouted after me, but they were too slow. Their voices quickly faded.

Gulls flew in circles high above. The path sloped uphill, through green grasses. *I'm running now, Dad. Are you happy?* Anger made my eyes sting. The coin flared hot in my pocket, though I'd left it on the table.

"Haley!" a woman's voice called, somewhere inside me. Had that voice cast a spell that consumed my mother, like Katrin had said, or had Mom really just run away because she knew that Katrin and Dad—

I ran faster, breathing hard, up some stairs and past the tourists at the Law Rock. By the drowning pool, Ari was scowling into the water. Anger pulled me past him, up the trail and toward the waterfall. I heard more words in my head, but they weren't in English, and I couldn't understand them. The pulling grew stronger. My anger burned hotter.

Fear trickled down my spine. I tried to stop running; my feet didn't listen. A pair of small birds flew out of my path. I heard the rush of the waterfall, but I couldn't slow down.

"Haley! I'm angry at them too, yeah?" Ari sounded very far away. He panted, as if he was running after me.

I reached the rocks and felt the cold spray of the waterfall. The pulling urged me around behind the stones, toward a dark cave within them. A raven cried out. Hot wind began to blow, and the scent of sulfur tinged the air.

The fear grew like fire beneath my skin. The cave mouth drew closer. I couldn't stop. I couldn't even turn around. I grabbed on to the stones. I couldn't turn back, so instead I tried climbing upward—anything to avoid going around the rocks and into that dark cave. The pulling fought me, but not as hard. I kept climbing, my sweaty hands sliding against the stone.

The voice inside me began yelling. My headache flared sharper. Down below, Ari called after me. I couldn't hear his words above the water. I could only keep climbing the slick rocks. Water soaked through my jeans and jacket, but I wasn't cold—I was stiflingly hot.

The world spun and went dark. I smelled smoke and the sour stench of old meat. I blinked my eyes open and found myself crouched in a dim cave. Long hair fell around me like a veil. I squeezed my eyes shut. The girl climbing the rocks seemed a distant vision. The ground trembled beneath me, a low murmur that began to build.

I didn't dare open my eyes. I knew when I did the vision would be gone, and I would be the long-haired woman in the cave.

Hot wind stroked my cheek. I jerked away from that burning touch. As I did, my sweaty fingers lost their grip on the stones, and I returned to my own body with a jolt. I was falling, falling—I reached for the rocks and missed. I screamed, even as fog filled the air. A hand grabbed at my pack and fell away. Cold wind whistled past my ears; wings beat the air. I braced for the pain that would take all other thoughts away.

I slammed into the rocks below, and the world went black.

⤳ Chapter 4 ⤳

I dreamed of a tower of gray blocks, stacked beside a rushing waterfall. Too high—a child's arm reached out and knocked the wobbling tower down.

I dreamed of a bow strung with fire. An arrow was loosed from the bow, and it caught fire as it flew, tracing a burning arc through the air. Where the arrow landed, I knew the world would burn, down to its very roots. I would burn, too, down to my very soul—but I didn't fear fire.

I dreamed of a gray-eyed girl who solemnly held out her fist to the man who knelt before her. "Promise me, Father. Promise I will determine my fate." She opened her hand. A ring lay there, woven of her own silken hair.

The man chucked her under the chin. "I'd promise

anything for my beautiful girl," he said. The child beamed up at him, but even in my dream I knew the man was lying. All fathers lied, one way or another.

The dream faded, leaving me alone in the dark. I tried to open my eyes. My lids were too heavy. Something had happened—there'd been wind, water, falling. There'd been pain, too, or would be once—

"You need not remember." The words held the rhythm of wingbeats, steady and lulling. I'd never heard that voice before. "You need only sleep."

I slept.

When I woke, I could open my eyes, but the darkness remained as thick as before. The air was cold and damp. Hard stone lay beneath my back. I tried to sit up.

Pain arced through my spine. It burned through my arms and legs and skull, my every shattered bone. I bit my lip to keep from screaming, remembering dimly that I must never cry out, however terrible my dreams. A gasp escaped my lips as I fell back to the stone.

"Not a good idea," said a squeaky voice. "You need rest. You need healing. You need time." I heard claws tapping stone. Something—the air around me?—lifted my head. Someone pressed a cup to my lips.

Warm, sweet liquid filled my mouth. I swallowed, and even that small movement hurt. Sweetness flowed down my throat, into my spine, along my arms and legs and skull, down to the smallest bones of my fingers and toes.

"Who are you?" My voice sounded strange and thick.

I heard a bark—or maybe a laugh. "Only a scrap of lingering lore some choose to remember. Nothing you need worry about."

I thought about sitting up again, but moving had *hurt* the last time I'd tried it. I struggled to remember what had happened, but thinking took too much work. I slept once more.

In my sleep, I heard voices.

A woman's voice: *"Haley! Where are you, Haley? The fire I called burns on—in my hair, in my thoughts, in the coin you yet hold. You took that coin of your own will. Do you refuse the bargain that goes with it? For three days I have returned to this cave, hidden from my father's view, to seek you out. Are you a coward after all?"*

A boy's voice: *"You are breathing. At least you are still breathing. I do not know where we are, but—I will find a way out of this place. I promise I'll be back."*

I tried to recall why I wanted a way out, but I saw only burning things: a bow, an arrow, a woman's hair, cracks within the earth.

A squeaky voice: *"Here. Drink this."* Sweetness filled me again.

A voice that held the beating of wings: *"You need not remember. You need only sleep."*

* * *

When I woke again, the pain was gone. I sat up slowly, afraid, but nothing hurt. I began trembling, with shock or relief or maybe both. The air was still dark. I couldn't see my own fingers, held up in front of my face. Just then, that didn't matter. "I'm all right," I whispered, and the trembling eased.

Small feet clicked against the stone and stopped beside me. I felt a cup pressed to my lips. The liquid within smelled sweet and alcoholic. I pushed it away.

"It would be better if you drank." The squeaky voice again. I reached out and felt soft fur. So soft—more like a plush toy than anything real.

"I'm not thirsty." Whatever was in the cup would make me sleep, and I didn't want to sleep anymore. I heard movement in the dark as the furred creature left my side. Something scraped the floor.

I felt around me. I was sitting on a hard low platform, like a stone bed. The air smelled heavy with water. I swung my feet over the edge—still no pain. "Is there light?" I asked my—captor? Rescuer? Had I needed rescuing?

"I will get light." Claws tapped rock, leaving me alone.

I squinted into the dark, but my eyes didn't adjust. I knew I'd been able to see before—where? I couldn't remember. My thoughts felt fuzzy and strange. I stood—the floor was stone, too—and walked forward, stretching my arms out in front of me. After a few steps I came to a rough stone wall.

My shoes squeaked as I returned to the platform. I'd been running. I remembered that much. I'd been running, and someone had been calling my name.

Haley—somehow, I pulled that name from the back of my mind. It was like pulling something out of thick, sucking mud. My name was Haley. I held on to the thought, afraid that if I let go, I would lose it.

I sank to my knees, fighting nausea. I was in more trouble than I could imagine if I had to work to remember my own name.

I rubbed my arms. They were covered in nylon—jacket sleeves. My long hair was loose, and it fell into my face. *Think, Haley.* Where did I live? I couldn't remember. Family? Nothing, just sludgy darkness where my memories should have been. My teeth chattered. It was cold in this stone room.

Yellow light flared at the edges of my sight. Too bright—I squeezed my eyes shut, then opened them. More light bloomed in front of me, behind me, as if by magic. The light cast faint shadows.

I blinked and stood. I was in a small stone room, maybe ten feet across, wearing jeans and a blue hooded jacket. The light came from small bowls of oil with burning wicks in them, set in shoulder-high niches in the walls. Smoke drifted from the bowls, carrying an oily animal scent. Aside from the bed and the lamps, the room was almost empty, with just an ivory-colored drinking horn filled with amber liquid, set in a wooden stand beside the bed, and some shelves and ledges in the walls, which disappeared into the darkness above me. To my left, a broad doorway led out into a dark tunnel.

A small white fox padded out of the tunnel and crossed the room to sit at my feet. An arctic fox with small ears and a long fluffy tail—not a red fox or a fennec fox or any of the other species names that tumbled into my awareness. Why could I remember twelve kinds of foxes when I couldn't remember my family or home?

"Light," the fox said.

Never mind what species he was—I sank abruptly down on the stone bed. "You can talk." None of those dozen species could talk.

"So can you." The fox scratched behind his ear with one paw. I couldn't help it—I reached out to pet him. The fox leaned into my hand. His woolly fur really was that soft.

Was I someone who liked animals? I stared into the darkness above. My name was Haley. What else? Mother and father? Sisters or brothers? My thoughts slid away when I tried to focus them, as if they, too, were beyond the light. I clenched my other hand into a fist, released it when my nails—sharp nails—dug into my palms. "Ouch!" I jammed both hands into my pockets.

My fingers brushed soft cloth in one pocket, warm metal in the other. A memory of gray eyes and hot wind shook loose from the dark, and another of losing my grip and falling—

I jerked my trembling hands out of my pockets. Maybe there was a reason I'd forgotten. I stared down at my palms. They were crossed with faint half-moon scars.

In the distance, I heard wings beat the air. A huge black raven flew out of the tunnel and into the room, wings outstretched. A half dozen small black-capped birds—arctic terns—followed in its wake.

I scrambled to my feet. The raven swooped up onto one of the ledges, perched there, and looked down at me through bright black eyes. Dizziness washed over me. Somehow I knew those eyes remembered all I'd forgotten. The smaller birds arrayed themselves on lower shelves while the fox tapped my ankle once—a friendly gesture— then curled up on the floor, wrapping his bushy tail around his paws.

The raven flapped its wings—slowly, rhythmically—and somehow those wingbeats shaped themselves into words. "So. You have chosen to wake." He flexed his black claws. His glossy wings shone in the lamplight.

"Who are you?" Speaking—thinking—took too much work while staring into those eyes. I looked down. My sneakers were gray with gravelly dust. "Why did you bring me here? What do you want?"

The raven's wings kept beating the air. I swayed in time to that beat. "I saved your life."

Even without looking at the bird, speaking took effort. "Why did my life need saving?"

"It didn't," the raven said matter-of-factly. "But the other one, by whose spell you were caught—the fire she called on could tear the land asunder, should it be set free. Perhaps your dying while bound to her magic would not be enough to release that fire. Perhaps it would. I prefer not to take chances. The other one was young when she cast her spell. She thought it a game, a matter of her own human life, yet the earth still trembles with the memory of how she called upon the realm of fire."

I had no idea what the raven was talking about, and my murky memories yielded nothing. "What other one?"

"I'll not name her, lest I give her more power—for though she died a thousand years before you were born, time is a fragile human thing and can be altered to bring the land's ending. All things must end, as my master foretold long ago. Even so I would hold off their end awhile longer. I would remember for a small time more."

"Wait, you're saying the world could end if I die?" *Yeah right, the earth really does revolve around me.* I laughed uneasily. I didn't need my memories to know how unlikely *that* was.

The raven didn't laugh. He just kept flapping his wings.

A chill breeze blew through the room. "This island, certainly, which is all of the world I can see. You are not as strongly tied to the spell as the other one. You have only touched the fire—you have not offered gifts to the giants who wield it, and they have not left their power burning within you in turn. If they had, you would be as far beyond my reach as the other one. As it is, the danger is smaller, but still real. Just ask the first victim of the spell."

"What first victim?" My throat caught on the words. There was pain in that question's answer, pain sharp as shattered bone.

"Ah." The raven's wingbeats slowed to a whisper. "Even were I willing to return that memory to you, you would not want it."

Yet now that I knew the memory—the pain—was there, I couldn't help searching my thoughts for it, like digging at an old scab.

The memory remained out of reach. I looked up again. It was easier now than before. I focused on the glossy wings and avoided the bright eyes. "Who *are* you?" My words echoed in the stone chamber.

"I have many names. Most of them humans have forgotten. Muninn is one a few yet remember. Memory is another. Not human memory—human memories are short. That is no matter. All any mortal beings once knew, I remember for them. Once I held those memories for my master, but he walks less and less often in this world. Yet though the old gods retreat to their own places, Memory remains in this land to the end of days."

I kept scratching at that scab. Pain shot behind my eyes, but I didn't cry out. I remembered how I'd woken, swallowing screams. Apparently I was someone who could handle pain. "I can hold my own memories," I said.

Muninn threw back his head and krawked—it sounded like a warning. "Your memories were small enough payment for the life I saved. What gift can you offer me to have them back again?"

I barely knew my name. What could I possibly have to give? Why should it take a gift just to get my own memories back? "You had no right to take them."

"Nor did I have any right to save your life. Yet save it I did, and that life is the one thing I'll not take back again." Muninn ducked his head and began grooming his sleek feathers.

The fox opened his tiny brown eyes. "It is easier to forget." The small terns bobbed their heads in agreement.

I shoved my hands into my pockets and felt warm metal once more. I pulled out a small silver coin, engraved with circles and lines. I heard—or maybe remembered—a woman's voice calling my name.

Muninn's head jerked up. His wings moved. "What is that? I remember that."

I held the coin out. "Would you like it?"

The raven blinked, his eyes flashing gray. "Now *that* is an interesting offer. Destroying the coin might make the earth safe from the spell—or it could release the spell's power into the world. Best, perhaps, if I simply keep watch over it to prevent you from drawing on its power."

"Take it, then." Even as I spoke, I knew I'd be glad to be rid of the thing. "Take it and give me my memories."

"I must think on this. I will return when I reach a decision." Muninn launched himself from his perch, circled me once, and flew from the chamber. The little black-capped birds flew after him. Only the white fox remained. He uncurled himself and stretched his front legs.

I sighed and sat down on the bed. "Do you have a name, too?"

The fox climbed up beside me. "You may call me Freki, if you like."

"I'm Haley."

"I know," the fox said, which seemed an unfair advantage. Why did everyone know who I was but me? Freki rested a paw on my leg and looked up. "Are you hungry?"

"Yeah." Starving, actually, though I hadn't realized it until then.

"I'll get food." The fox walked over to the drinking horn. "Are you going to finish this?"

I shook my head, though my throat was dry. "It's drugged, isn't it?"

Freki's ears flicked back. "It is not drugged." He sounded

offended. "But it is, perhaps, stronger than mortals are accustomed to—strong enough to mend broken bones and torn flesh. My master sustained himself on such mead. Will you finish it?"

I shook my head. I was glad to be mended, but I didn't want to sleep again. "No. You can have it, if you want."

The fox looked at up me, small brown eyes bright in the lamplight. "Are you certain? Even my master never allowed me a sip of his sacred mead."

"Yeah, I'm sure. Enjoy."

Freki lowered his nose into the horn, making quiet lapping sounds as he drank. He was surprisingly tidy. He didn't spill a single drop. He licked the last bits out with his long pink tongue, and I laughed.

Freki didn't seem to mind. He nudged my hands with his warm nose. His breath smelled faintly of alcohol. "A most excellent gift. I will not forget it." He turned and walked from the room, the tip of his bushy tail brushing the floor behind him. He didn't seem sleepy, just a bit more careful in his steps than before.

I lay back on the stone bed, staring up into the shadows. "My name is Haley," I whispered. How could everything I knew end there?

Freki padded back in a short time later, a small drinking skin hanging on a string from his neck. Behind him, two small birds flew in together, a plate piled with food hovering in the air between them. They flew to the bed, and the plate gently set itself down beside me. The terns made squeaky clicking sounds as they left the room, and their long tail feathers fanned out behind them.

The smell of cooked meat made my stomach rumble. Freki bowed his neck so I could take the skin. It hovered above the ground a little, too. "For later," Freki said. "In case you change your mind."

"I won't change my mind." I set the skin down beside the bed. "You don't have any water, do you?"

Freki's white whiskers twitched. "What adult drinks water?"

"This one." When you lived in the desert, water tasted better than coffee, better than soda.

The desert. I wrenched that thought free from the mud of my thoughts. *I live in a desert.*

"I would not offend a guest with watered-down wine, let alone water itself. Do you require anything else?"

I shook my head and took the plate in my lap. Freki curled up beside me. I reached out to stroke his fur. The fox made a small contented sound and rolled over so that I could get his belly. The white fur there was just as soft.

Only after my hand was covered with fox fur did I realize Freki hadn't brought a fork. I wiped my fingers on my jeans as best I could, took a slice of meat in my hands, and bit into it. It tasted like lamb, only sweeter. As I chewed, the sweetness grew stronger, making my whole body tingle.

Shit. "You drugged the meat, too." Already my voice sounded thick. I threw the plate across the room—too late. The cave blurred around me. I tried to stand but felt myself falling, toward stones that suddenly seemed soft as feathers.

"Can I have your meat, too?" a voice squeaked. I was asleep before I could answer.

⌐ *Chapter 5* ⌐

As I slept, the voices returned.

A girl's voice: *"Teach me sorcery, Uncle. I promise I won't tell."*

A man's voice: *"Are you strong enough, Hallgerd? Stronger than the power you would command?"*

The girl: *"You do not know me, Uncle, if you doubt my strength."*

The man, laughing: *"Oh, I know you well enough. Gladly I will teach you."*

I knew awful things would come from that teaching, and I tried to call out a warning. My lips wouldn't move. I saw gray blocks tumbling down, flames consuming them as they fell.

A boy's voice: *"Wake up, Haley. Please wake up!"*

Someone shook my shoulder. I rolled away. I wanted to keep sleeping.

Light shone into my face. I cursed and blinked. Green eyes stared down at me—a boy in a black leather jacket, wool cap jammed over his ears. He had a backpack slung over one shoulder and a small blue LED keychain flashlight in his hand—the one he'd shone into my eyes. The lamps were still lit, the oil no lower than before. Where the boy's light hit the stones, it seemed more green than blue.

"I found a way out of here." His voice held a trace of an accent. I couldn't tell from where. He grabbed my hand. I drew it away as I sat up.

"Do I know you?"

The boy scowled, as if he didn't have time for this. There were weary circles around his eyes. "Yeah, I'm Luke Skywalker, and I'm here to rescue you." I gave him a blank look, and he rolled his eyes. "Of course you know me. It's Ari, remember?"

The name meant nothing to me. My breathing sped up. Panic hovered right behind. Just how much had I forgotten?

"Okay, maybe you're angry at me, too," the boy—Ari—said. "Why should you be different from anyone else? But we must leave while we can. I don't think I am even supposed to be here, only when the birds came, I got swept along behind you. I'm still not sure how it happened—there were wings and wind, and then the dark and the cave."

Was Ari a friend? Boyfriend? He was awfully cute, in a shaggy sort of way. We had to be important to each other or he wouldn't want to rescue me, right? I stared at the way his brown hair fell into his face, but my memories remained lost in darkness. The darkness pulled at me, grasping for the few things I did remember. I pulled back, breathing hard, and got to my feet. Fear rippled through me. "I'm sorry. I can't remember."

"Can't remember what?"

"Any of it."

For a moment Ari didn't seem to understand. Then his eyes went wide. "A raven. Yes, of course. There are stories about ravens." He grabbed my hand again. This time, I let him. His grip felt comfortable in mine, like maybe we'd held hands before. "Please, Haley. We have to get out of here."

"Where *are* we?" My throat was parched. I'd have killed for a drink of water.

"I am not sure. I have some ideas, but they're even crazier than my mother's ideas. All I know is we don't belong here. Maybe you will remember once we leave?"

I brushed my other hand against my pocket, feeling the coin's warmth through my jeans. Would Muninn accept my offer? "I'm making a bargain for my memories."

Ari tugged at his hat. "I think there is no bargaining with the powers that live here. Not if they are real. And if they are not real, they cannot help us."

From down the hall, I heard the beating of wings. Ari stiffened, and his fingers tightened around mine. Was Muninn after his memories, too?

The raven swooped in and hovered before us. "Oh, I'm real enough, boy. More real than any human child." Ari's light wavered in his free hand. The raven's feathers shone blue-black. "Did you think I did not know you were here?"

I pulled my hand free and put myself between Ari and the bird. Muninn had already said he wouldn't take *my* life. A half dozen terns swooped into the room and arrayed themselves on the ledges.

"Don't be stupid." Ari stepped around to face the raven.

I moved to his side. "Leave him alone."

Muninn landed on the floor—the top of his head was well past my knee—and stared up at me through tiny black eyes. I grew dizzy, stumbled, and cast my gaze to the floor. "You barely have coin enough to bargain for your own memories, yet you would bargain for his life as well? Humans change so little. Always you think to command more power than you have." Muninn's gaze shifted to Ari. "So what do you think, boy? Shall I hold your memories for the next thousand years?" The raven walked slowly around us, claws clacking against the stone. He reached out a wing to brush the edge of Ari's jacket. "Or shall I make you remember instead?"

"You don't scare me." Ari's voice shook—he *sounded* scared—but his accent was gone.

"You wish to know fear? That's easy enough." The raven raised his wings, then lowered them, hard and fast. Cold wind gusted through the chamber. I barely felt that wind, but Ari staggered back. His eyes grew large. I grabbed his arm, steadying him. He jerked away with surprising strength.

"Remember, boy. Remember why your father's ancestors wore that bearskin coat long ago. Remember!" Muninn raised his wings a second time, and a third. Ari's jacket began to melt, dripping down his legs like hot plastic. Again I reached for him. He scrambled away. Liquid leather flowed around his hands and feet, through his hair. He grabbed for his zipper, but suddenly it was gone, and his hands were too large, anyway, his fingers all the wrong shape.

"Ari!" The cry hurt my dry throat.

He fell to his hands and knees, backpack sliding to the floor. "Run," he whispered, his accent back, his voice hoarse.

No way was I leaving him. "Stop it!" I told Muninn. The raven made a low clicking sound, like laughter, and kept flapping his wings.

The jacket had completely engulfed Ari. His body stretched like clay within it—nose pulling into a long snout, ears shrinking back against his head, black claws sprouting from his strange flat hands and feet. My heart pounded. He'd tried to *rescue* me.

White fur sprouted from black leather. He was growing now, impossibly fast—impossibly large. He lifted his head and roared. The sound echoed off the stone walls and reverberated deep in my chest.

He was a bear. A huge white polar bear, his shoulders as tall as mine. Only his eyes were human, the same bright green as before. Nausea washed over me. I stepped toward him, then froze as polar bear facts flooded my brain. Polar bears were one of the few predators who wouldn't hesitate to attack humans. Red blood stained their white fur when they fed on seals and walruses and other arctic prey, anything they could find.

I backed away, but I kept focusing on those human eyes. "Ari?"

The bear raised his enormous paws and leaped at the air. When he landed, he broke into a powerful loping run and disappeared down the hall into the dark. The small birds flew after him, squeaking and clicking all the way.

I ran at Muninn. The raven flew up out of my reach. "Turn him back!" Whoever Ari was, he didn't deserve this.

Muninn landed on a ledge with a krawk, and I knew he was laughing at me and Ari both. His wings lazily beat the air. "Would you give me your silver coin in order to make the boy forget his warrior ancestors once more? Or do you still seek to trade for your own memories? I have made my decision. I will accept your gift, but the coin will only buy so much. Decide, Haley."

I couldn't leave Ari trapped as a bear. Yet I couldn't leave myself trapped forever without my memories, either. "Would you take the coin in exchange for just freeing us both?"

"You are not prisoners," Muninn said. "I deal in memory, not bindings. I cannot hold you here without your consent. Yet I'll not help you find a way out, not for a far greater gift than you offer. Time is fluid in this cave, not firmly bound to the outside world. As long as you remain here, the bond between you and the other one is muted. Should you leave, you would surely meet her again, though none can say when, in your life or hers. I will not risk seeing you harmed by that meeting. I'll not risk seeing the fire set free."

I reached into my pocket. The coin was warm. I remembered holding it as I stood by the edge of the sea—the memory slipped out of my reach as I grasped at it. I clutched the coin harder and remembered other things, bits and pieces with nothing to connect them.

Myself, running down a cactus-lined street, dusk smudging the sky and a hot desert wind brushing my skin. I ran for the joy of running, but also to forget.

A man in an airport, walking toward me. His battered backpack was slung over his shoulders, and his face looked as crumpled as his clothes. I looked past him, searching the crowd for someone else, though I knew I wouldn't find her.

A woman with long blond hair and a long red cloak. "Haley," *she whispered.* "Come here, Haley."

A boy—Ari—throwing down a menu and opening his mouth to speak—

The coin flared hotter, burning me. I jerked my hand free, leaving the thing in my pocket. Whatever Ari had been about to say, I didn't want to hear it.

"So you see," Muninn said, "you do not wish to remember."

Remembering hurt. I rubbed at my palm. Should I turn the coin over to Muninn? Tell the raven to turn Ari human again and leave my memories safely hidden away?

Yet my few broken memories told me that I could handle the hot desert wind. I could handle the pain of broken bones without crying out.

"We have no bargain." My memories were somehow tied to that coin. With it, maybe I could get them back on my own. Without it, my memories would still be gone—and I'd have nothing left to bargain with.

Muninn's claws flexed against the stone. "You do not want the coin. If you remembered, you would know."

"But I don't remember." I looked right into his eyes, not flinching as dizziness washed over me. I could handle lots of things. "If you want to negotiate further, you'll have to give me my memories."

Muninn launched himself from the ledge, claws aimed right at me. I ducked. He circled once around the room, then disappeared down the tunnel with an angry krawk.

"We have no bargain!" I called after him.

And I had nothing at all, save for an old coin and a scrap of cloth and a few scattered memories.

Something brushed my ankles. I looked down to see Freki winding around my legs. I hadn't seen him enter the room. "What do you deal in?" I asked the little fox bitterly.

"Only companionship. Muninn and I may share a master, but we have different roles to play."

I had no more reason to trust him than Muninn, but still I knelt down and squeezed him tightly. The little fox didn't resist, not even when I found myself sobbing into his thick musky fur.

I didn't have time for crying, not now. Ari—the bear Ari had become—was still out there. With a shuddering breath I drew away. "Can you turn Ari back?" I asked the fox. "Can *you* give me my memories back?"

The tip of Freki's tail brushed the floor. "I do not deal in memory. I'm sorry, Haley."

"Can you at least help us get out of here?"

Freki looked at me through sympathetic brown eyes but said nothing. I was on my own.

Ari's flashlight lay on the floor, casting a beam of blue light. I turned it off and put it in my pocket with the cloth. His backpack lay on the floor, too. I took it to the bed. Maybe there'd be something inside I could bargain with. Freki climbed up beside me, watching as I unzipped the pack's small outer pocket. "Will you at least not try to stop me?" I asked him.

"I can no more bind you than Muninn can," the fox said.

That was something, at least. I went through the pack. The outer pocket held a thin wallet and a United States passport. I opened the passport. Dark brown eyes—almost black—stared at me from beneath blond hair pulled into a high ponytail. My own hair was unbound, but I pulled a lock around, and it was the exact same color. This wasn't Ari's backpack—it was *mine.*

Haley Martinez, the passport read. I'd been sixteen when it was issued, and there was only one stamp inside, saying I'd entered *Island*—Iceland—on June 21, but not that I'd left again.

Why was I visiting Iceland? As I tried to remember, a headache stabbed behind my eyes. I let it go—for now—set down the passport, and opened the wallet. It held a few multicolored bills and a handful of silver coins with fish stamped on them. Ordinary coins, cool to the touch. Freki sniffed them without much interest. Did that mean Muninn wouldn't be interested, either?

There were some photos in the wallet: a man with his

black hair sticking out in all directions, grinning atop a rocky pink outcrop; a gray-eyed woman in a white doctor's jacket, a small orange cat in her arms, one of its legs bound in a bright turquoise bandage; myself, standing beside a serious-looking boy with short dark hair, a large yellow-and-black king snake draped over our arms and linked hands. I guessed the man and woman were my parents, but who was the boy?

There were no pictures of Ari. Maybe the pictures were out of date. Maybe I'd always meant to take one of him.

I looked down the dark tunnel. What if I never got to take that picture? What if the boy who'd tried to rescue me was gone forever, turned to white fur and black claws?

No. I wouldn't let that happen. *Whoever I am, no way do I give up that easily.* I opened the main inner pocket of the pack. It contained a small yellow notebook, an English-to-Icelandic phrase book, and beneath them—

Water! Freki sniffed disdainfully as I uncapped the bottle and took a long swallow. Cool liquid soothed my parched throat. I'd never tasted anything so wonderful—or maybe I had and didn't remember. I forced myself to screw the cap back on before I drank it all.

I also found a smushed bag of malt balls. My stomach grumbled at the scent of half-melted chocolate. Freki nosed at the bag. I gave him a malt ball—he took it between his paws and nibbled it delicately—then gulped down a handful of my own. The grumbling eased. I put the malt balls back into the pack beside the water and opened the notebook. A note was written on the first page:

> *Haley,*
>
> *I've done my best to translate these pages. Your father will tell you the words written here are nonsense, but you must believe me when I say the danger is real. If we are lucky, that danger will not find you—but I will not rely on luck. I will not let you face this magic unarmed.*
>
> *I am sorry you could not stay home. I am sorry for what happened to your mother. I am sorry for many things.*
>
> *By the time you read this, we'll have already talked. But call if you need to talk more.*
>
> *Whatever happens, you can always call me.*
>
> *Katrin*

Another name. Another person I couldn't remember. Had Katrin tried to rescue me, too? There was a phone number beneath her name.

What had happened to my mother? How could I forget something like *that*? I turned the page.

Warnings from Thorgerd, daughter of
Hallgerd and Glum, passed on to her
daughters in turn:

Never run from magic.

When offered escape, turn away, no matter
how deeply you desire it.

Take some of the fire if you can, but do
not take too much. Do not let the fire
consume you.

If the spell lands on you in spite of these
warnings, you must cast it back again.
Go to Hlidarendi to return the coin from
whence it came.

The means of the casting, plus other useful
spells, follow.

The rest of the pages were covered with strange symbols—squiggles and circles and lines—with smaller writing scrawled among the symbols.

Had I run from magic? Was that why my life had needed saving? I reached into my pocket and drew out the coin, hoping that holding it would help me remember, like before.

Heat shot through my palm—too hot! I dropped the thing and it clattered to the ground. I pressed my hand to my mouth as the burning cooled.

On the floor, the silver coin shone in the lamplight. I didn't dare lose it, no matter how much it burned. I reached into my other pocket for the cloth. A white handkerchief streaked with dried blood. My blood? I used the handkerchief to pick up the coin. The heat was fainter through the cotton.

I felt a powerful tug, as if the coin was trying to pull me from the room. For just a second, I caught an image of a boy with shaggy hair and a wool hat jammed down over his ears. The coin kept tugging. Leading me toward Ari?

My heart pounded. Not letting go of that coin for a second, I loaded everything into my pack. The wineskin Freki had brought me still lay beside the bed. No way was I drinking the mead, but if I found more water, I could use the skin to carry it. I tugged the cork free, meaning to empty it out.

Freki let out a single sharp bark and rose to his feet. "Don't spill that! My master would not like it!"

"I thought your master didn't walk in this world anymore."

Freki made a strange sound, low in his throat. "And if you're wise, you'll not draw his attention back to it. If you spill his mead—if you deny his hospitality by letting it touch the earth—he will know."

Right. No point pushing my luck. I corked the skin and put it into the pack. Maybe I could empty it later, when I got out of here.

Memories or no memories, I'd get Ari and myself both free. I zipped and shouldered the pack, took Ari's flashlight in my other hand, and followed the coin's pull into the dark.

∽ *Chapter 6* ∽

The tunnel was colder than the room. I pulled up my hood and zipped my jacket to the chin. The flashlight's thin beam cast eerie blue light on the tunnel walls. Water dripped somewhere up ahead, and the air felt thick and wet.

Freki followed at my heels, to guard me or provide companionship, I didn't know. Either way, his presence was comforting. Was that a sort of magic, too?

The tunnel branched left. The wrapped coin pulled me forward. I followed, but as I passed the branch, a gust of icy air blew toward me. A child's voice whispered, *"Three shells in return for my poem, poem, poem."* The words echoed off the stone walls.

I stopped short and peered down the side tunnel. "Hello?"

"*I'll toss my silver at them and watch them fight, fight, fight.*" An old man's voice, carried by the same cold wind. I turned left, though the coin urged me away. There were pictures on the tunnel walls. They skittered like nervous lizards out of my sight as the light hit them. *A boat torn apart by the sea. A coffin washing to shore.* I squinted into the distance. I saw no old man, no young boy.

Teeth nipped at my ankle. I looked down and saw Freki's mouth around my leg. "You hear memory, nothing more." He drew back, the tip of his tail brushing the floor.

"*The sea has stolen my sons.*" The echoing voice *sounded* real—real and incredibly sad.

"Muninn holds all the island's memories here," Freki said. "Follow them without purpose, and you'll wander to the end of days and still not find your way back to where you began."

I clutched the handkerchief-wrapped coin tighter. Bad enough to lose my memories—I didn't want to spend my life lost among other people's memories instead. "That's a lot of tunnels."

The fox's whiskers twitched. "Only Iceland's memories lie here. Other lands have their own guardians and their own mountains."

A brief image flashed through my thoughts: jagged brown mountains beneath a hot blue sky. *My* mountains, I somehow knew. I tried to remember, but the mountains sank into the muddy darkness of my missing memories,

leaving behind empty shells of words—mountains, desert—
with no images to go with them. My eyes stung. Muninn
had no right to take who I was away from me.

I brushed my eyes, turned my back on the voices and
the images on the walls, and let the coin lead me on, back
to the main tunnel. Freki walked alongside me, his gait
smooth and liquid. The tunnel branched again and again.
Sometimes the coin urged me left, sometimes right, sometimes straight ahead. I counted the turnings, repeating them
to myself to make sure I could get back.

"*I have spun twelve ells of wool. You have killed a man.
A fine morning's work for us both.*"

"*I already must grieve for my brother. Is it not enough
for you that I set a bowl of porridge before his killer?*"

My hand clenched around the coin. I fought the urge
to stop, to listen closer, to try to stare longer at the moving
pictures on the tunnel walls. Scraps of mist drifted through
the air, raising goose bumps beneath my jacket. Were all
the memories in this place of sadness and loss?

"*My father gone, my brother gone, only this price upon
my head remains.*"

"*Yes, the girl is beautiful, and men enough will suffer
for it, but I do not know how the eyes of a thief have come
into our family.*"

The coin flared suddenly hot. Smoke rose from the
handkerchief. A woman's voice, not in the tunnels but in

my own head. *"How dare Hrut speak of me that way!"*
Anger in those words. A moment's silence, then, *"Haley?"*

Dizziness washed over me. *The other one,* I thought. The
one whose spell had caught me. I ran from that turning, not
sure what I was so scared of. My legs trembled, then settled
into an easy lope, as if I was used to running. The light
bobbed ahead of me. The coin cooled from hot to warm. I
kept going, enjoying the feel of my feet hitting stone and cool
sweat trickling down my neck. Had I liked to run before?

In the distance, I heard a roar. I quickly slowed back to
a walk. I was breathing hard, but that felt good, too. Freki
caught up with me as the coin pulled me sharply left.

Up ahead, the tunnel ended abruptly. The bear—Ari—
huddled against the far wall, his nose hidden beneath his
enormous legs. My blue light shone on his white fur. Two
terns perched on the ledge above him.

He looked up, through eyes that seemed more blue than
green by my light, and growled.

"You may want to stop here," Freki said.

"Yeah. Good idea." I stopped, though the coin kept
pulling me toward the bear. Did it *want* to kill me? Mist
curled past the beam of my light. Around me I heard the
memories of other roars and growls. The hair on my arms
prickled at the sound.

"Are you still in there?" I asked Ari. He kept staring at
me. He was trembling—maybe he was as scared as I was.

Yeah, but it's not like being trapped with a scared polar bear is a good thing. I looked at his long black claws. My light wavered, shining off the walls. I saw images of bears in battle, tearing through warrior shields and chain vests as if they were paper.

"Any ideas?" I asked Freki.

Freki wrapped his tail around his legs. "I am no spellcaster, and even if I were, it is not my place to interfere."

I remembered something from the notebook in my pack. *Other useful spells follow.* Freki was no spellcaster, but what about me?

The coin kept urging me on. I stuck it in my pocket, keeping only the handkerchief in my hand. The pulling continued. It wasn't the coin that wanted to kill me—it was the handkerchief. *I should drop it and run away.* How could I make a bear remember who he really was when I didn't know who *I* really was?

Was I the sort of person who would run away? I seemed pretty good at running. Was I the sort of person who'd abandon someone who had tried to rescue me? Who maybe cared about me, and who maybe I cared about in turn?

To hell with who I was. That's not who I am.

The bear kept growling. I shoved the handkerchief into my pocket and pulled the notebook from my pack. Freki lay down and buried his nose beneath his fluffy tail, watching me all the while.

By the flashlight's blue beam I flipped past the pages I'd

already read. *A spell for restoring one's own memories,* the next page said. I hesitated, but the spell required a raven's feather. Maybe I could find some way to steal one from Muninn—later. I turned the page.

A spell for returning berserks to their true form, whether they will it or no. "Berserks?" I said aloud. "Like crazy people?"

Freki lifted his head. "Warriors with animal shapes. Very powerful. My master valued them. Fearsome in battle, ill suited to life outside of it."

The bear didn't look like a warrior, pressed against the wall like that. I quickly scanned the spell.

Berserks do not respond as readily to runes and chants as others do to magic. Still, you may try reciting these words and see if the shifter wishes to change back.

The words that followed were a mix of familiar and unfamiliar letters. I had no idea how to sound them out. There was a bit more English at the bottom of the page, though: *Alternately, you may offer the berserk some item that belongs to him, and see if it reminds him of his human life.*

I dropped the spellbook and yanked the charred, bloody handkerchief from my pocket. "Was this yours?" Was that why it had led me to him? Had my backpack led Ari to me, too? Did objects remember, in some strange way, who they belonged to?

I started toward him, holding the handkerchief out in

front of me, while the birds on the ledge watched through tiny eyes.

"You have a warrior's soul," Freki said, but he made no move to follow me.

Here, kitty, kitty. I kept walking, fighting nervous giggles, until I was close enough to reach out and touch the bear's nose—if I had a death wish. I reached toward him. Ari snarled. I dropped the handkerchief at his feet and skittered back.

With surprising care, the bear drew the thing between his paws. He sniffed it with his long nose, as if it were a book he was reading. He made a questioning sound and looked up.

"You still there, Ari?"

A ripple ran along his body, like wind on water. Fur retreated into black bear skin, claws into paws. Skin turned to clay once more, and beneath it the bear shrank, paws melting into human hands, snout into a human face. That skin drew away from legs and arms and face—

All at once Ari knelt gasping before me on hands and knees, wearing his leather jacket and jeans. He looked up at me, his eyes wild, his whole body shivering. The hair beneath his wool cap was bright white, not brown like before. The birds took off from the ledge, chittering harshly as they disappeared down the tunnel.

Ari tried to get up. His legs wobbled and he crumpled to the ground. I knelt to take him in my arms, my own body trembling with relief. Holding him felt familiar and right. Surely I knew this boy. "You're all right." I held him tighter, until his shivering eased.

He looked up at me. "Thank you, Haley." He had an incredibly sweet smile. Our faces were just a few inches apart.

I felt like I was still being pulled. I did what felt right, even if I couldn't remember why. I pulled my hood back, leaned down, and brushed my lips against his. Surely—yes—I'd done this before.

Ari drew away a moment, as if still frightened. Then he drew closer. We pressed our lips together while the damp air raised more shivers from us both. I reached beneath his hat and ran my fingers through his hair. It felt coarse and soft at once. I shrugged off the backpack and let the flashlight drop from my other hand. That hand brushed my pocket. The coin felt warm through the denim.

A fragment of memory: *A dark-haired boy—the boy in my wallet photo. We kissed beneath the bright desert moon while hot wind blew all around and we promised we'd e-mail each other every single day. The boy was shorter than me, and my hands cradled his head. I drew back to look down at his quiet brown eyes—*

I jerked abruptly away from Ari and groped for the flashlight. I shone it toward him. He smiled, but then his green eyes grew uncertain.

"How long have I known you?" I hoped he'd be hurt that I could possibly forget him.

Ari looked down as if embarrassed, and my stomach knotted up. "Time passes so strangely in this place. Sometimes it feels like we've been here a few hours, sometimes like years—" He shut his eyes. "That is not what you are asking."

"Before we came here." More than anything, I wanted to draw him closer again.

"Yes, of course. That would be—perhaps a day."

"One *day*?"

"To give me some credit, I did not start that kiss."

My cheeks burned hot. "You could have stopped it!"

A sheepish smile crossed his face. "Yes, but I am not stupid."

"And you think I *am*?" I scrambled to my feet. Freki looked up and cocked one ear quizzically.

"No, of course I don't think that. . . ."

My lips still tingled. I feared if I spoke at all, I'd begin kissing him again, and that wouldn't be fair to either of us. Or maybe it would be fair. Maybe I'd broken up with the desert boy months ago.

I *had* to get my memories back. I couldn't spend the rest of my life like this.

"I did not stop because I did not want to stop," Ari said slowly, "but also because I thought you did not want to stop. I am sorry."

Great. He had to go ahead and be nice about it. I grabbed his handkerchief from the floor, wiped my stinging eyes, and handed it to him. He shoved it into his pocket. I stuck the spellbook in my backpack and pulled the pack over my shoulders. "You said you know a way out of here?" Once we were out maybe I could find a raven's feather—a normal non-talking raven's feather—and try the memory spell. Or maybe my memories would return on their own once we were away from Muninn.

"There are some problems. But yes." Ari got to his feet, gave a small gasp, and fell again.

I helped him back up. "Sorry," he said. "Sorry, I—"

"It's not your fault," I snapped, doing my best to ignore the warmth of his arm as he leaned on me.

Around us, the memories of other bears, of other times, growled softly. "I think I am not quite used to being human again." Ari's white hair—and eyebrows and eyelashes—made his face seem very pale. He shuddered. "I did not know it was possible to forget such a thing."

Apparently it was possible to forget all sorts of things. I steadied him as we hobbled down the hallway. At least he was okay. We'd deal with everything else later.

"If you can get us back to the place where you slept," Ari said, "I can find the way from there."

I shone the flashlight back the way we'd come and played all the turnings in my mind. "This way." I hoped Muninn wouldn't be waiting for us when we got there.

Ari kept leaning on me as we walked. Freki followed at our heels. Ari gave the little fox a suspicious look, then shrugged and walked on. Memories whispered around us, none of them mine.

An old woman's voice: *"I must to bed, but ale for all, and enjoy yourselves as you will."*

A young woman's voice: *"Take me abroad with you, for it is not Iceland that I love."*

A small smile crossed Ari's face. "I know that story."

"Did he take her?" It was clear enough the young woman spoke to a lover.

Ari stopped and turned to me, his expression strange. "I did not think you knew Icelandic. Have you been—how do they say?—holding out on me?"

"It's not in Icelandic." But I listened harder. The words were different from the words Ari and I spoke with each other, even though they made just as much sense.

Ari scrunched his pale brows together. "Can you hear me now?" he asked, all trace of accent gone from his voice.

"Sure." Only after I spoke did I realize we'd both used that other, not-English language.

"Did I speak both languages before?" I asked in slow, careful English.

"Not that you told me," Ari answered, still in the other language. "You tried to speak Icelandic once, but your accent was terrible. Now it's just—a little odd. Old-fashioned, maybe?"

Freki nudged the back of my knee with his nose. "It is my master's mead." The little fox spoke Icelandic, too, though something about his intonation was different from Ari's. I realized I'd been speaking Icelandic with Freki, as well, and with Muninn—automatically answering in whatever language I was spoken to in.

"Your master—" Ari stopped short to stare at the little fox.

"My master no longer walks in this world," Freki said.

"Well, that's *something*, at least." Ari looked like he was trying to figure something out. "Aren't you and your brother supposed to be wolves?"

Freki's whiskers twitched. "There are no wolves in Iceland," he said matter-of-factly.

Ari grinned at that. "Yeah, well, remind me to tell my teachers. I'm sure they'll be very interested. So Haley drank—the mead of poetry?" He sounded like he was trying to get his brain around a difficult idea. That made two of us. How could some drugged alcohol teach me a whole new language—not to mention mend broken bones?

"Even my master's mead can only do so much. Given the gibberish Haley spoke when she arrived here, it's a wonder we got her speaking intelligible words at all." Freki flicked an ear toward me. "You'll have to handle the poetry on your own."

"I'll cope." I kept using Icelandic so Freki would

understand. "Do you have the mead of memory lying around someplace, too?"

Freki's whiskers twitched again—because he thought that was funny or because there really was such a thing, I couldn't tell. "You're no help," I told him.

The little fox stretched his legs out in front of him, unconcerned.

"And they say Icelandic is hard to learn," Ari said wryly. "If it's all the same to you, I'll stick to my own language from now on. English is not so easy for me, you see."

His English sounded awfully good to me, but what did I know? Not much, at the moment.

"If Haley doesn't want that mead next time, you can give it to me," Ari told the fox. "I'll give you poetry complete with a solid bass line."

Freki didn't answer that, just headed down the hall ahead of us. I thought of the mead in my pack. Ari probably wouldn't be half as interested in it if he knew it would put him to sleep.

He gave a rueful laugh. "And to think I once told my mother all her sorcery talk was nonsense. If we make it out of here, I owe her an apology."

I heard a whisper of memory—in my head, not in the air around me. "But you said it wasn't sorcery you were sorry for."

A pained look crossed Ari's face. "You remember that?"

I tried to remember more. My thoughts slid away;

my head began to hurt. A drop of water dripped from the ceiling and trickled down my jacket. "What *were* you sorry for?"

Ari drew a sharp breath. "See, answering that question is one of the things that got us into this mess." He pulled away from me. "Thanks, Haley. I think I can walk on my own now."

I missed the weight of his arm on my shoulders, but I didn't say so. I gripped the flashlight tightly as the tunnels whispered on. *"Take me abroad with you, for it is not Iceland that I love, love, love."*

"Of course he didn't take her with him." Ari scowled. I couldn't tell whether he was angry with me or himself. "He went abroad and flirted with the pretty Norwegian girls, and so she married his best friend instead. And then both men died. A tragedy, just like in Shakespeare."

I'd gone abroad, too. Had I left someone behind? More water dripped in the distance. "What happened to the woman? Did she die, too?"

Ari shook his head, white hair falling into his eyes. "Nah, she remarried and lived to a ripe old age."

What kind of romance was that? A bit of mist floated past the beam of my light. "Didn't take her long to get over him, did it?"

"What makes you think she got over him?" Ari plucked a strand of hair from beneath his cap, squinted at it, and frowned. "It's not that simple."

But it was simple: Either you loved someone or you didn't. Yet as if to mock me, the air around us whispered, in the same woman's voice, *"Though I loved him best, I treated him worst."* Ari laughed, a pained sound.

In the distance, I heard the faint beating of wings. I froze and switched off the light. Ari's shallow breathing seemed loud beside me.

Freki twined around my legs. "There are no secrets here," the fox said. "Muninn knows where you are, just as I do, and he comes or not as he chooses."

The wingbeats grew closer, then faded. I waited until they were completely gone before I turned the light back on and continued walking, Ari close by my side. I wanted to reach for him; I clenched my free hand into a fist instead. Nails dug into my palm. I forced my hand open before they could break skin. Why did I keep *doing* that? You'd think I wanted to hurt myself. I glanced at the scars there and wondered if I did.

We reached the final turning. I shone the light down one last tunnel and saw a round room with a stone bed at its center. The room was empty, no raven waiting for us there.

"Right. I can take it from here." Ari took the light. He glanced suspiciously at Freki, then back at me.

I shrugged. "He says he won't try to stop us."

"Is that true?" Ari asked him.

The little fox silently stared up at us with his small brown eyes.

"Yeah, you expect us to trust you just because you're cute, don't you?"

Freki didn't answer. Ari laughed to himself and started walking. He led us past several familiar turnings, then turned sharply right. I followed him, Freki a silent white shadow at my side. We began a steep climb. Ari panted with effort, but my legs made their way uphill easily enough, as if used to working hard.

Images flickered around us. The voices whispered on. *"You shall not hew!"* one of them said.

"Like in the *Lord of the Rings*," Ari muttered.

I remembered that movie, and the book, too. Only there the line had been, "You shall not pass!" which wasn't the same at all. Great—I could remember lines out of old movies but not whether I had a boyfriend.

"Hey, weren't Arwen and Aragorn twentieth cousins, too?" Ari laughed softly. He glanced at me, but I had no idea what he was talking about. He quickly returned his gaze to the sloping tunnel.

Whispers of vengeance and battle gave way to whispers of bad weather and lost grazing, of failing crops and starving livestock.

"I have committed no crime. A charm to keep foxes from lambs, nothing more!"

Freki sniffed disdainfully. "There is no charm that can keep a fox from a lamb."

"Hear my innocence. By God and Christ I swear I used sorcery against no man."

On the walls I saw images of flames lapping at wood and skin. I saw a woman bound and thrown into deep waters.

A memory flickered through my thoughts: *A pool of water, turned bloodred by the sun.* The memory slid away as I tried to focus on it. I bit my lip to keep from crying out with frustration. Maybe it'd be easier to remember if I began with the small things, the ones that didn't matter so much. TV shows. Old movies. Like *Lord of the Rings* or *Star Wars*. "Hey!"

Ari looked back at me.

"You are so not Luke Skywalker!"

Ari's mouth quirked. "You prefer Han Solo, then?"

"I . . ." I didn't know. I remembered *Star Wars*, sure, but I didn't remember whether I *liked* it, or the actors in it. I remembered only the parts that had nothing to do with me. When I tried to get at what I'd actually thought about anything, I hit more darkness. I wanted to scream. Instead I gave a shaky laugh. "You're not Han Solo, either."

"Ah." Ari nodded knowingly. "That leaves only Darth Vader, then."

Chill mist drifted through the air around us, thicker than before. "Darth Vader was kind of cute when he was younger," I said. At least, I thought so now—who knew what I'd thought before?

"Darth Vader was a jerk when he was younger," Ari said without heat.

"As opposed to his old age, when he had a productive career blowing up planets?"

Ari laughed, and the sound echoed off the walls around us, making the corridor feel just a little less cold than before.

We reached a dead end. Ari shone his light on the wall, and I saw depressions in the gray stone, evenly spaced, like a ladder. Ari put the flashlight between his teeth and began to climb. The light faded above me. I found the first foothold as much by feel as by sight.

I felt claws through my jeans. Freki scrambled up my legs, over my backpack, and onto my shoulders. He was heavier than he looked, but I didn't kick him off, whether because he really was cute or because I'd grown used to his company, I didn't know. His fur was soft against my neck.

My arms were nowhere near as strong as my legs. They strained as I climbed. The voices and images faded away. The wall disappeared into the mist below. Dizziness washed over me, and I turned quickly back to the cold stone I was climbing. Apparently I was someone who was scared—terrified—of heights. I remembered falling through empty space, water roaring in my ears. My head swam. My grip loosened on the stone.

Claws dug into my shoulders. "Ouch!" The memory fled and I quickly tightened my hold.

"Thank you, Freki." I was breathing hard. The fox nudged my neck with his damp nose.

I didn't look down again, just focused on finding handholds and footholds, on climbing higher and higher, following the blue beam of Ari's flashlight above me.

The light vanished. My breath caught, but then the light returned—Ari knelt on a ledge, pointing it down at me. I kept climbing. Freki leaped from my shoulders onto the ledge. I followed, shaking out sore arms.

Ari led the way up a low staircase and into another stone room, like the room where I'd slept, only larger. He swept his light around the space, which held no mist at all. There was a small stone bed, covered with furs, and a huge wooden door—a door!—carved with a pattern of arcs and lines. No handle, no doorknob—but a door was a start, right? *We just might make it out of here.*

Ari's light moved on, to a stone desk covered with scraps of parchment and more animal skins, a wooden staff—carved with symbols—leaning against it. An old man sat in a wooden chair there, head on his arms, asleep. Ari's eyes grew large. He quickly shut off the light. I guessed the man hadn't been here when Ari found this place—or maybe that was one of the "problems" he'd mentioned. *Pretty big problem, having a guard at the door.* In the dark Ari grabbed my hand and pulled me back toward the stairs.

I heard a sound like wood scraping stone. It echoed and re-echoed through the chamber. "Who disturbs my sleep?" a voice boomed.

Heavy footsteps strode across the floor, right toward us.

~ Chapter 7 ~

Light bloomed from niches in the walls. Ari and I whirled around, racing for the stairs, but then we heard wingbeats down below.

Right. No going back that way. We turned to face the man. His brown beard was streaked with gray. His wool cloak hung open over a belted shirt and baggy pants wrapped with strips of leather. His eyes swept quickly over Ari and took on a calculating look as they focused on me.

"That one is no friend to foxes," Freki whispered at my feet. I guessed that meant the man wasn't Freki's master. The little fox nudged my leg with his nose, then slipped back into the shadows.

The man stepped toward us. Ari edged closer to me.

Behind us the sound of wings beat on. "And who might you two be?" The man's voice was lazy and slow, as if he were used to having all the time in the world. He glanced back at Ari. "Your hair is white for one so young."

Ari straightened beside me, though his hand was sweating in mine. "I am Ari, Katrin's son. This is Haley, Gabriel's daughter." *Gabriel—my father?* "Who are you?"

"Svan is my name. Bjorn's son. I guard this place in return for my lodging here." He took another step toward us. I stepped back and nearly stumbled over the top stair. Ari grabbed my arm, steadying me.

He looked at the man. "Svan like in the saga? Surely not."

The man laughed, though his gaze didn't leave us. "Do they yet remember this old sorcerer out in the wide world?"

"Remember is one way of putting it," Ari said.

Behind us, the wingbeats grew louder. My heart pounded. We had to get out of here. I stepped toward the door, not that I expected it to be that easy.

Svan grabbed his staff and stepped in front of me, blocking the way. He poked my chest with his free hand. I shoved him away, glaring.

Svan laughed again. "Haley. Are you sure we haven't met before?"

I wasn't sure, but I wasn't about to tell him so. *Try that again and you're going to get kicked where it hurts.* Ari made a low sound that reminded me of his bear's growl. "Haley is an American. A—a Vinlander, you might say."

I couldn't tell whether the words—American or Vinlander, whatever that was—meant anything to Svan. A pair of terns flew chittering into the room, landed on Svan's desk, and watched us.

"Please," Ari said, the politeness obviously forced. "We need to leave this place."

The sorcerer chuckled. "I can see you are the sort of man who would rather bargain than fight, Ari, Katrin's son." *Was that an insult?* "Tell me what gift you would offer in return for your freedom."

Ari hesitated, then squared his shoulders and stepped forward. "A poem," he said.

I looked at Ari. He shrugged uneasily. "It works in the sagas," he said in English.

If Svan understood English he gave no sign. He tilted his head as if intrigued. "Very well. Let's hear your poem, boy."

Two more small birds swooped into the room and perched in niches in the wall. Ari switched back to Icelandic, looking right at Svan as he recited:

> *This isn't real, it's just an old story*
> *Lies and betrayals, words stab like swords*
> *Birds cry out, someone's running away*
> *No one in stories heeds dusty old warnings.*

This isn't real, it's just an old story
Footsteps that stop at the end of a path
The ones left behind, they keep the lies going
In stories there always are prices to pay.

This isn't real, it's just an old story
The pages all crumbling, the ending a mess
Stories don't stop at the end of the summer
And magic has never solved anything yet.

Images flashed through my head at Ari's words: feet running over gravel, a raven crying out, the rush of water. Svan stared at Ari, as if considering his poem, but then he threw back his head and laughed. "You price your words too high, boy. You'll have to do better than that!"

I glared at Svan. "*I* liked it," I said.

Ari looked down, and his neck flushed red. "I don't have anything else to bargain with."

"Oh, I wouldn't be so sure about that." A slow smile crossed Svan's face. He reached out and grabbed my arm.

I tried to pull away, but he was stronger than he looked. I kneed him in the groin, hard.

Svan grunted and let go, doubling over. His staff clattered to the floor, but he didn't stop smiling. "A strong woman. I like that." He winked at Ari. "What do you say? A gift for a lonely old man? Long have I been in this mountain. She'll more than buy your freedom."

I tensed, ready to kick him, even as my eyes scanned the room for a weapon. The sorcerer straightened.

Ari shone the flashlight right into his eyes. Svan threw a hand up over his face and staggered back. He wasn't smiling anymore. "You're only a boy, whatever the color of your hair. You wouldn't know what to do with her!"

Ari growled softly. In my pocket, the coin flared with heat, burning through the denim. Heat was a weapon—I grabbed the coin. Memory washed over me.

A golden-haired girl and a man—Svan—sitting together on a black beach. The man drew circles and arcs and lines in the dark sand, and the girl carefully copied each symbol— each rune—in turn.

"See, Uncle, I can learn."

"Yes, Hallgerd. Now do it again."

"I already understand! Don't you trust me?"

The coin burned hotter. I flinched, and it fell clattering to the stones.

"I *do* know you." Svan's voice brought me back to the present. He looked at me through slitted eyes, then held his hands out in front of him, as if to show he meant no harm. *A bit late for that.* "Your eyes are wrong, but you are surely Hallgerd's kin."

The distant wingbeats fell silent. Ari still held the flashlight, aimed just below Svan's eyes now. A listening silence filled the room.

The sorcerer reached for the coin. I snapped it up—it was still warm, but not as hot as before—and shoved it into my pocket.

"The runes inscribed there are clearly my niece's work," Svan said. "How did it come to be yours?"

Damn good question. "Who's Hallgerd?" Even as I asked, I knew: *The other one, who Muninn wouldn't name.*

"Hallgerd was a bitch." Ari's eyes never left Svan— Hallgerd's uncle. "She's also someone you don't want to mess with."

"Aye, she is that." A strange sadness crossed Svan's features. He picked up his staff. "Teaching Hallgerd was a mistake. She combined the runes in ways I never intended, and in so doing called on fires that yet threaten the land beyond these stones. I think it is not by chance that you've come to me now." He nodded. "It is time to undo my mistake. I will leave with you, Haley, and teach you the sorcery with which to end Hallgerd's spell."

"Hell no," Ari said.

Muninn hadn't seemed sure the spell *could* be ended. "You'd let us both leave if we let you come with us?" I said. That seemed way too easy.

Svan glanced sidelong at Ari, and I knew there'd been no *both* in his original bargain. He nodded. "Yes."

"It's the best chance we're likely to get," I told Ari in English, though I didn't want Svan hanging around any more than Ari did.

"You'll keep your hands to yourself," Ari told the sorcerer in Icelandic.

"She is my kin!" Svan looked offended. He gestured at Ari with his staff. "What do you take me for, boy?"

"I do not think you want me to answer that," Ari muttered darkly in English.

Svan laughed and strode across the room, ignoring the birds perched on the table. He fastened his cloak closed with a round silver pin—a snake eating its own tail—then wrapped a strip of leather inscribed with more runes around his staff.

He walked up to the door and pounded the floor three times. The sound echoed through my chest, loud as Ari's polar bear roar. The sorcerer chanted:

> *By the sweat of the trolls, open!*
> *By the blood of men, open!*
> *By the voices of the gods*
> *And those who serve them, open!*

Svan blew softly over the staff. The door swung silently inward, revealing a patch of gray sky beyond.

Wingbeats burst into the air. The little birds launched themselves right at us.

"Run!" Svan said.

I grabbed Ari's hand and raced across the room, ignoring

the pack slamming against my back and the bird claws grabbing at my hair. A darker shadow swooped into the room. The little birds flew away. Ari and I kept running, through the open doorway. Icy air hit us, way colder than in the cave. We skittered to a stop.

We stood on a stone ledge only a few yards across. To our right the ledge quickly narrowed and disappeared, leaving only a vertical stone cliff. To our left the ledge wound around the curve of a towering black mountain.

Ahead of us, where the ledge fell away, there was only gray swirling fog. I stepped back, fighting dizziness. Ari grabbed a stone from the ground and threw it into the fog. It disappeared silently into the mist, but I didn't hear it hit bottom. Ari's eyes widened, and he moved back, too. Svan stepped out to join us, his staff in hand and a leather sack slung over his back. The drop into nowhere didn't seem to bother *him*.

"Not wise, Haley." Muninn's wingbeats were slow and rhythmic behind me. The raven swooped through the doorway and turned to hover before me in the mist. As I looked into his shiny eyes, my hands fell limp by my sides, even as some small part of me kept thinking about that drop. Fear shuddered through me. *I was falling, arms flailing for a hold, knowing when I landed I would die*—I wrenched my thoughts away from that memory.

"You do not want to remember." Muninn's wings kept pumping the air. "You do not want to return to the world that nearly destroyed you. I cannot bind you, but I can give you one more chance. Turn back before the door closes."

Maybe Muninn was right. Maybe it was better to forget. I stepped back into the doorway. My thoughts felt fuzzy and strange. Another step and I'd be inside.

Ari grabbed my hand. "Don't." He held on so tightly, as if all by himself he could keep me from taking that step. His palm felt warm against mine. I wanted to remember *him,* even if we only had a day together for me to remember. If I turned back, what he meant to me would always be a mystery.

I walked back out of the doorway. Ari let out a breath, but he didn't let go of my hand.

Muninn screeched his anger. "I cannot bind you, yet I will do what I can to keep you from acting in the wide world. Know this, Haley, Amanda and Gabriel's daughter, and Ari, Katrin and Thorolf's son: None shall remember you, beyond these stones. None shall see you, comfort you, aid you."

He turned his gaze to Svan and I stumbled, released from the raven's hold. "As for you, sorcerer," Muninn said, "you know well enough the price for failing to guard the door. No more will you wander these tunnels, listening to the past and learning its magic. In the human world you shall age and die, like the mortal you are. Now go!"

Muninn gave one final sharp beat of his wings. A bitter wind began to blow. The raven swooped past us and disappeared into the cave, his wingbeats echoing. "I leave you alone, alone, alone."

"Not so alone as all that." I felt fur brush against my jeans. I looked down, wind biting my cheeks, and Freki looked up at me. "Thank you for the mead, Haley. Good fortune go with you." I reached down to scratch the fox behind the ears. He slipped out of reach through the wooden door. It swung shut as it had opened, without a sound.

I searched my thoughts, but still found only darkness in place of my memories. Amanda and Gabriel—my parents— when I searched for images to go with them, I saw only the lifeless pictures in my wallet. Leaving Muninn's mountain hadn't changed anything.

"So," Svan said. "That went better than expected." Staff in hand, he brushed past us, following the ledge like a trail away from Muninn's door.

"I don't trust him," Ari whispered.

Neither did I, but what choice did we have? It wasn't like there was anyplace else we could go. I followed Svan. Still holding my hand, Ari walked by my side, only a couple of feet from the edge. Looking at the fog made me all trembly. I forced my gaze away. To my left, the mountain rose steeply, a solid, comforting presence.

The wind picked up. Icy raindrops blew into my face. Svan disappeared around the mountain's curve. Ari and I walked faster. The sorcerer glanced back as we came into view. "What do you wait for? The mountain will not remain in the mortal realm for long."

"What's that supposed to mean?" Ari asked.

Svan looked at him like he couldn't believe how stupid Ari was. "Now that would depend on the realm, wouldn't it? In the realm of fire, your flesh will melt and boil; in the realm of ice, it will freeze and shatter; in the realm of light, you will turn to sunbeams and disappear. In other realms, other things. I suggest we not wait around to recite them." He walked on, his staff tapping the ledge, which had begun to slope downhill.

The cold rain fell harder. I pulled up my hood, but the wind blew the rain right into it. More rain dripped from Ari's hat. I glanced past him, toward the foggy emptiness— and quickly wrenched my gaze away, breathing hard.

"Haley?" Ari squeezed my hand, and I realized I'd stopped walking. I looked up at the mountain. The vertical rock wall stretched up and up—that made me dizzy, too. I squeezed my eyes closed. When I opened them Ari was looking at me, his own eyes wide with concern.

"I fell, didn't I?" I said.

Ari frowned and began walking again. I followed,

keeping my gaze firmly on the stone beneath my feet. Svan had disappeared out of sight once more.

"Were you there when I fell? Did you see?"

Ari pulled his cap down over his ears. "Yeah. I tried to stop you, but I messed it up. So Muninn saved your life instead and I got pulled along for the ride."

Ari wasn't the one who'd fallen. He couldn't have messed up half as much as me. "Why did I fall?" It seemed suddenly important to know.

Ari walked faster. I hurried to keep up, still keeping my eyes on the ledge. "You climbed too high," Ari said. "And then you let go. I don't know why."

The ledge grew slippery as the rain continued. I glanced at my scarred palm. I couldn't have let go on purpose, could I?

Svan had stopped walking. A couple dozen paces ahead of him, the ledge ended abruptly, giving way to more fog. A few cold tendrils drifted toward us.

"Now what?" I said.

"Now we jump," Svan said, as if that should have been obvious. He broke into a run, his leather shoes slapping the stone. As he reached the edge he held his arms out wide—one hand holding his staff, the other his leather bag—and leaped into the fog. It swallowed him at once, leaving no sign he'd been there.

In the silence that followed, Ari and I stared at each other. Dizziness washed over me, stronger than before.

I began backing away, only Ari still held my hand. After a few steps I came to a halt.

The blowing rain stung my cheeks. *I can't,* I thought, but I had no choice. I looked up at Ari. "You go first," I said.

"And give you the chance to change your mind? No way."

My hand trembled in Ari's grasp. "Someone has to go first," I said reasonably.

"We'll jump together," Ari said.

We wouldn't jump as far together. Ari was risking his own life just to make sure I didn't risk mine. I adjusted the backpack on my shoulders, knowing I was stalling. "We'll have to run first. We should count. But you don't have to—"

"One!" Ari ran, dragging me along.

I stumbled, then matched his pace. "Two!" I said. *I can't do this.*

"Three!" Ari said. "Now!"

We jumped, our hands still clasped. Wind whistled past my ears as fog surrounded us. It blew my hood back, and my hair streamed out behind me.

The whistling turned to a roar. Icy rain gave way to burning wind. Somehow, impossibly, we were still jumping. The fog around us turned to roiling orange flames. Heat rolled over me, a physical thing. *The realm of fire.* Something reached for me out of the flames—a huge misshapen arm, made entirely of flame. Hot fingers stroked my cheek. Any second my skin would catch fire, and then there would be pain—

Another fiery arm reached for Ari. "Leave him alone!" I screamed, knowing they couldn't hear me, knowing they wouldn't listen if they could.

Yet in my head, through the roaring, I heard a rough, inhuman voice, crackling like dry paper. *"What would you give us to leave him alone?"* Burning eyes stared at me through the flames. A burning shudder ran through me.

"Anything!" I said, knowing I had less to offer the power here than I'd had to offer Muninn.

Fiery fingers brushed my hair. *"Once before, we accepted such golden locks as a gift. We accept them now. We gift you our fire in turn. Nothing will stay our power this time. You will take our fire into your blood and not merely your hair. You will take our fire into your world, and in so doing, perhaps help us find our way free into that world at last. Do you accept?"*

Hot wind scoured my skin like sandpaper. A sickening charred smell filled the air—my own skin melting away. The darkness in me burned away, too, replaced by light so bright it hurt my eyes. Another moment and I'd burn down to ash. I clutched Ari's hand, though I could no longer see him through the burning. "Yes!" I said, knowing only that I wanted the heat to go away.

"Very good." The voice in my head made a satisfied sound. The smell of burning hair filled the air.

I slammed into ice-cold water. It cooled the fire, leaving behind warm coals that settled down somewhere deep inside me. Water washed over me as my hands and knees hit wet sand. I sputtered to my feet, thigh-deep in salt water, my clothes and backpack soaked through and dripping. A hand grabbed mine—Ari. He must have landed on his feet; he was only wet to the thighs. "Haley, your hair . . ."

The fire was gone, my skin unburned. We were no longer on a mountain ledge, but in a bay beside a black sandy beach. Beyond the beach I saw a dirt-and-gravel road, beyond that, gray hills smudged with red and orange mosses.

Ari shivered—was he cold? His hat was gone. Rain dimpled the surface of the bay, and water soaked through my sneakers, but I wasn't cold at all. Ari splashed out of the water, and I followed, still holding his hand. As we reached the shore, I stopped short and stared at him. "I know you," I said.

Ari kept shivering. "Yes, we've been through this already. I'm Ari, Katrin's son—"

"No. I *remember* you. I ran into your dog—" I reached around and touched my hair. It was short, barely touching my ears and the back of my neck. The ends were brittle—burned away—and the smell of burning hair lingered. The darkness over my memories had burned away, too. I was Haley, I went to Rincon High, I studied biology and wanted to work with animals and ran track, my father was Gabe, my mother was Amanda—

My mom—I released Ari's hand, my fingernails digging for my palms. My mom had disappeared—no, she *hadn't* disappeared, she'd been caught by a spell—it had to be a spell, because I knew magic was real now—only before the spell caught her she'd run, because she found out that Dad had—nails broke through my palms, the pain shoving other thoughts away. Smoke seemed to rise from the broken skin, but I could have imagined that. I knew only that I had one more chance to push the memories back, to bury them so deeply that only the stone halls of Muninn's cave would ever remember them.

I forced my fingernails away from my skin. The pain receded, the smoke disappeared—if it had ever been there—and I faced the memory straight on. "My dad," I said slowly, looking at Ari. "And your mom . . ." *Katrin, who gave me her notebook, who told me not to run . . .* "They had an affair. My mom found out, and she ran." Ari looked down, as if my steady gaze hurt him. He rubbed his sleeves for warmth. His lips were pale, which should have worried me, but I just went on, "Mom's been gone a year. I came to Iceland to find her. If Katrin's right, there's nothing left to find. Hallgerd's spell—" Katrin said the spell had consumed

Mom, as surely as the fire Ari and I had leaped through had almost consumed us.

The coals inside me grew hot at the thought. My jeans and jacket steamed in the damp air. I reached for the coin—its metal felt merely warm now—and closed my fingers around it.

The coin flared hotter. The ground shook beneath me, and I fell to my knees.

"Haley!" Hallgerd's voice roared into my head. This time, I understood every word. *"Where have you been?"*

~ *Chapter 8* ~

A woman stood before me, gray eyes smoldering, blond hair swirling like flame around her, so long it pooled at her feet. Her red cloak was bright against the gray sky. She reached for me, but I drew away.

"I waited for you. For days I returned to the cave. When I could no longer return I searched from my home, whenever I could escape the eyes of my family. I sought you on my wedding day, and past it as well, until Thorvald was gone and my anger was quenched. All that time you hid from my spell. Why do you wake it now, after all these years?"

The coin burned against my hand. The air held the stench of sulfur. *It hasn't been years,* I thought. The woman shimmered, as if with heat. For an instant the air seemed to blur, and I knelt—not in a cave this time but on a yellow autumn hillside, beside a wooden house with a grass-thatched roof. I wrenched my focus back to the woman and the beach. My eyes hurt, the way they do when you try to make a fuzzy picture clear, but I didn't let the picture go. I stared at Hallgerd—at Svan's kinswoman, who had killed her three husbands, and who Katrin thought had also killed my mom—yet no one *knew,* because Mom had never been found.

Hallgerd reached toward my singed hair. I felt a hot shudder as her fingers passed right through me. *"You are either very brave or very foolish to gift so much of yourself to the realm of fire. I gave them but a few dozen strands when I cast my spell."*

The ground still shook, but that seemed a small thing. I'd come here for answers. I looked right into Hallgerd's gray eyes. "What did you do to Mom?" Nothing mattered more than the answer to that question.

The earth went still. Hallgerd frowned. *"She accepted my gift. But then she ran, and the spell consumed her. I did nothing. She did everything."*

"You killed her." I waited for Hallgerd to deny it.

"Indeed." Hallgerd met my gaze without shame. *"What compensation will you seek for this, Haley?"*

"Compensation?" How did Hallgerd imagine there could be compensation for such a thing? "You can leave me the hell alone, is what you can do!"

Hallgerd laughed. *"You price your mother's life far too*

low. Thorvald has been dead many years, and my second husband as well. I desire escape no longer. I'm content to live and die by Gunnar's side. Gladly I'll leave you alone. I release my claim on the coin—and on the spell. Do with them as you will. Farewell, Haley."

Hallgerd faded away. I dropped the coin, scrambled to my feet, and lunged at her. "Get back here!" My hands grabbed someone's shoulders. I began shaking them, shaking hard, and only when I shoved the person to the sand did I realize it wasn't Hallgerd.

Ari looked up. His lips were blue now, and his teeth had begun to chatter, but an ironic grin crossed his face. "It'd be easier—if you could remember—who I am."

Not funny. I scrambled away from him. My mother was gone, and he was making a joke—a stupid joke. I began coughing, dry empty heaves. *Gone.* I'd come to Iceland to find my mother, but there was nothing left to find. Tears ran down my face, hot as the fire that had burned my hair away.

It was Mom who'd always talked me out of cutting my hair. Mom who'd held me after nightmares, who'd kept my life from falling apart a million different ways. Nothing had been as hard as the year she'd been gone. I coughed harder. My chest ached. Nothing could make this right. *Never, ever, ever.*

I felt Ari's hand on my shoulder, and I jerked away. "You knew!" I screamed. He'd known she was gone for a whole year, while I waited and hoped and fought off nightmares, telling myself that the worst possible thing couldn't be the true thing.

"I thought my mom was crazy." Ari shivered harder. I heard him, didn't hear. "I wanted her to be crazy, about this at least."

My nails dug for my palms, but it wasn't enough. I rolled up my jacket and dug my nails into my arm. Still not enough—I couldn't seem to break skin. I dug harder, waiting for the pain of hot flowing blood.

"Haley!" Ari grabbed my wrists. I fought him, and as I did a hot sulfurous smell filled the air. The coals in me flared hot, heat roaring through me as I struggled. The fire roared outward, toward the one who held me. The ground shook.

"Bloody *hell*!" Ari dropped his grip. I fell backward onto the sand. A few raindrops landed on my face, but they didn't feel cold. My clothes were still steaming. I saw red welts on Ari's palms as he staggered back.

You will take our fire into your blood. Sweat trickled down my neck as I remembered the words. *You will take our fire into your world.*

"What have I done?" I whispered. I thought of the heat in Hallgerd's coin, but the fire inside me had nothing to do with her spell. It came from my own bargain with the fire creatures. *Once before, we accepted such golden locks as a gift.*

I thought of the winter storms back home, how they

doused the desert's summer heat and turned dry washes to cold flowing rivers. I thought of cold rainwater rushing over my bare feet. The fire—and the anger—inside of me subsided down to banked coals.

Ari shoved his hands into his pockets, green eyes wary. "You okay?" he asked, shivering still.

No, I'm not. Okay was part of some other world, the world I'd lived in before my mother went to Iceland, before I'd known there was any such thing as magic.

Ari's skin was icy pale. How could he be so cold? I barely remembered what cold felt like. "Your arm," he said.

My arm stung, but when I looked down, I saw only the fading imprints of my fingernails—no broken skin, no blood. I pulled my sleeve down to cover it. My palms had bled, just a little, but the wounds were already clotted over. Had I really seen smoke there? What did it mean to take fire into your blood? "I'm fine," I said.

Ari drew his hand from his pocket and reached for mine. His palm was still red. I'd burned him without half trying—that's what taking fire into your blood meant. I didn't take his hand.

Soft waves lapped at the shore. Ari stared at me, teeth chattering, body trembling. Whatever he was looking for— reassurance?—I couldn't give it to him. I couldn't even promise I wouldn't burn him again. I still felt warm coals somewhere deep inside me.

At last Ari pointed into the distance. "I think maybe—the

sorcerer—has started—a fire." I followed his gaze. A faint orange glow shone against the gray hills.

Like I needed a fire. I had all the fire I needed within me. *Would that fire consume me as it had consumed Mom? Would that be such a bad thing?* my treacherous thoughts asked me.

Hell yes. If the fire destroyed me, there'd be no one left to make Hallgerd pay. Somehow she had to pay for this.

Wind picked up, cutting right through my jacket. I barely noticed, but Ari shuddered. "Please, Haley. It's cold—out here. Let's go—to—the fire." He started toward it, and I followed. Where were we, anyway? Not Thingvellir, though the gray hills and black sand did look volcanic. Back in Iceland, at least?

The sand gave way to the dirt-and-gravel road, which was slick with water. The rain fell harder. The wind grew stronger. We bent our heads into it. Water streamed from Ari's white hair and black leather jacket.

The wind began to moan. The fire turned to a faint orange smudge through the blowing water. Ari stumbled and fell.

I helped him up. "I'm all right," he said, but his breath came out in gasps. I felt a ripple of fear. *He'll be fine. I just need to get him to the fire.* He leaned on my shoulders as he staggered on.

The road gave way to sucking mud. We climbed a short

slope, ducked beneath a craggy overhang, and then we were beside the fire. Svan was sitting there, staring into the flames—ordinary flames that couldn't speak. "Took you long enough," he said, not looking up.

Ari made a rude gesture as he sank down beside the fire. His shudders turned violent as his rain-soaked jeans began to sizzle and dry. With shaking hands he unzipped his jacket and pulled it off, moving closer to the flames to let them dry his wet skin and clothes.

I shrugged off my sodden backpack, pulled off my jacket—the hood had burned away along with my hair—and drew Ari close, rubbing my hands along his bare arms to warm them. Svan winked, as if my not wanting to see Ari die of hypothermia meant I was ready to jump into bed with Ari. Which of course I wasn't, because I was dating Jared—I pushed that thought aside. *One thing at a time.* I hadn't gotten us out of the fire realm only to have Ari freeze to death in this one.

"You're warm, Haley." Ari moved closer to me, even as he kicked off his muddy shoes, pulled off his socks, and set them by the fire to dry. "How can you be so warm?" His shivering subsided. "Some rescuer I am, yeah?"

"Couldn't have made it without you, Luke."

Ari laughed at that. Beyond the overhang, I heard a clattering sound. Hail, pounding the gravel and mud. Wherever we were, we weren't leaving anytime soon.

Even if we were back in Iceland, where would I go, anyway? Back to Dad? What happened to Mom—it was Dad's fault, too. I shivered, not because of the cold. Ari's arms tightened around me.

Svan chuckled. "I'm sure your father will find a good match for you when you're ready for a real man. Until then, there's no harm in playing."

I nearly told the sorcerer what he could do with himself, but it wasn't like I wanted to go back into that storm.

Svan handed us a couple of strips of dried meat from his bag. I bit fiercely into mine. It tasted like old cardboard—rubbery old cardboard—but I kept chewing. So did Ari. Had he had anything to eat in Muninn's cave?

"I don't suppose you brought any drink?" Svan asked as he finished a strip of meat of his own.

Like I wanted him drunk. A gust blew beneath the overhang. The fire flickered, but Svan made a quick hand gesture over the flames, and they steadied and burned on. I felt some spark deep within me yearn toward those flames.

Svan looked sharply up. Did he feel the spark as well? He reached toward my singed hair. I jerked away. No way was I letting him touch me. Ari stiffened beside me.

"A bit close," Svan said. "You should have walked faster. The realm must have begun to change to fire as you jumped."

No *begun* about it, but I didn't tell Svan that. I still didn't trust him.

He fed a piece of damp driftwood to the fire. It hissed, but then the wood caught. Flames leaped toward the stone above us. "Do you still have Hallgerd's coin?"

I'd dropped it—but I drew away from Ari and reached into my pocket. The coin was there, warm against my fingers. Would I ever be free of it? No matter what I did—dropped it, threw it away—the thing always found me, just as it must have found Mom.

The coin—Hallgerd's spell—had *killed* Mom. I clenched my hand around the silver.

"We must destroy it," Svan said. "Only by destroying the coin can the fires Hallgerd called on be contained."

Muninn had thought it best to hide Hallgerd's coin away in his cave, because destroying it might only make things worse. Katrin thought we needed to bring the coin to Hallgerd's home and return it, but I didn't exactly trust her anymore, either.

And I didn't want to give *anything* back to Hallgerd. "Will it hurt her much, if we destroy the coin?" Hallgerd said she'd released her claim on it—maybe that didn't make any difference. She was still the one who'd cast the spell.

Svan wouldn't meet my eyes. "What matter that, if it keep Hallgerd's fire from burning the world?"

You don't understand. "Will it hurt her a lot?" *Because right now, I'm more than okay with that.*

"It might," Svan admitted, his gaze on the fire.

"Good," I said.

Ari and Svan both looked at me. "Truly, you are Hall-gerd's kin," Svan said.

Ari scowled, showing what he thought of that. He didn't understand, either. A stray raindrop landed in his hair. "If destroying the coin will hurt Hallgerd, what will it do to Haley?"

Svan loosened his cloak. "Hallgerd altered my teachings in ways I did not anticipate. She always thought she understood more than she did. I cannot say for certain what will happen. Destroying the coin could destroy all those bound to it."

"It doesn't matter." I'd risk myself a hundred times if only I could make Hallgerd suffer.

"The hell it doesn't." Ari pressed his lips into an angry line. Outside, the wind began to blow the rain sideways.

Svan raised his voice to be heard over it. "I believe Haley makes this choice willingly."

"No," Ari said. "Don't, Haley."

Easy for him to say. "Your mother's still alive."

Ari flinched, then looked right at me, his green eyes sharp.

Ari and his mom were Hallgerd's kin, too. Why should my mom be dead, while his mom was just fine? Especially since Katrin was the one who had—what? Slept with Dad? Only messed around a little? I didn't want to know. *It was easier when I didn't remember.*

How could Dad have even thought of cheating on Mom? What sort of jerk was he? I thought of how lost he'd looked when he came home last summer. *Funny how you left out the part about how it was your fault, Dad.*

"We'll take what precautions we can," Svan said, "but given the liberties Hallgerd took with her spell, I can make no promises."

Ari drew his jacket back on, staring at me all the while. "If you need someone to blame, Haley, blame me and be done with it."

"You didn't—"

Ari picked up a gray rock and turned it in his hands. Outside, the wind and rain continued. "I came home early, okay? From my summer job. I opened the door, and there they were together. It's not like Mom hasn't had other boyfriends, but none of them were *married.* The worst part was how Gabe and Mom kept saying it was none of my business. The hell it wasn't. I was so angry." Ari drew a breath. "One day I'll learn to keep my big mouth shut."

"So you walked in on them." I quickly pushed the images *that* brought up out of my mind. "That doesn't make it your fault."

Ari flung the rock out into the storm. "Who do you think told your mother? Do you think my mom and your dad just walked up to her and confessed?" Sparks flew up from the fire. Svan shut his eyes, but his shoulders remained stiff, watchful. "I thought Amanda had a right to know," Ari said, quieter now. "I am such an idiot."

"She did have a right to know." My voice was low, too, almost too low to hear over the wind.

Ari shook his head. "You don't understand. She got so angry. She just couldn't stop yelling, while your dad—"

"Got really quiet." My throat felt suddenly tight. "I know."

"Who could blame your mom for running?" Ari said.

I can. Smoke stung my eyes. *Because she ran from me, too.*

"Your dad thought she just needed time to think, only she never came back. And then my mom, she started looking at the earthquake patterns—there was a decent-sized quake, you know, the day Amanda disappeared—then went down by the waterfall, found a place where some footsteps ended—and began going on and on about Hallgerd and sorcery. I thought it was just another excuse. Mom had all sorts of excuses, like when she told me your parents were thinking about getting divorced, anyway—"

"*What?*"

Ari scowled and threw another rock out into the rain. "See? I never know when to shut up. I thought you knew."

"No." Mom and Dad fought, sure, I knew that—but

they weren't getting-a-divorce fights. They'd never talked about getting a divorce.

How could I not have realized, anyway? "I am so stupid."

Ari's mouth pulled into a rueful smile. "So you see, we have something in common."

It doesn't matter, I told myself again. All that mattered was that Mom was gone. That was Dad's fault, and Katrin's, but most of all it was Hallgerd's.

I looked at Svan. "Do you have any spells to bring back the dead?"

Svan opened his eyes, and I knew he'd heard our every word. "You need a body to bring back the dead."

Hallgerd hadn't even left me that much. I glared down at the coin I held. The fire in me rose toward it. Funny how I could feel so much heat, when every time I thought about Mom, everything in me felt like cold ashes.

The ground trembled a little, as if in response to the fire—my fire or the coin's fire, I couldn't tell.

Svan raised an eyebrow. "So you see, Hallgerd's spell remains active."

Ari scowled. I ignored him and shoved the coin toward Svan. "Hell yes, I want to destroy it."

Svan nodded. "As soon as the storm ends, I'll gather the necessary supplies. We shouldn't waste any time. There's no knowing what my niece's magic will do."

What about my magic? I kept the thought to myself. "The sooner the better," I told Svan. I'd cast any spell, if there was a chance that Hallgerd might feel it. If there was some chance I could hurt her as much as she'd hurt me.

Nothing matters as much as that, I told myself. *Nothing.*

~ *Chapter 9* ~

I *dreamed I held a bow made of fire. I dreamed I drew back the bowstring and released an arrow.*

Flames leaped from the string, catching my skin, my hair. Fire roared through me. I knew then that I was the bow, the string, the arrow. Fire consumed me as I flew through the air. So much fire—but I also knew better than to scream—

I woke with a gasp, drenched in sweat. The air was calm, the storm gone. I heard water lapping at sand and saw the overhang above me.

I didn't remember falling asleep. Ari's leather jacket was draped over me; he lay curled by my side, shivering in his *Star Wars* T-shirt. In the thin light, his hair and face both seemed very pale. Svan was nowhere in sight.

Ari muttered something about ravens and dawn's light in his sleep. It sort of rhymed and sort of didn't. I sat up and moved to drape the jacket over him. I still couldn't feel the cold.

Ari jerked awake, looked up at me, and frowned. "Don't do this," he said.

I didn't have to ask what he meant. "Hallgerd killed her. I can't just let her get away with that."

"Hallgerd's been dead a thousand years. For all that time, everyone's remembered how horrible she was. Isn't that punishment enough?"

"No." *Nowhere near enough.* And she wasn't dead for me, not when I'd only just spoken with her.

Svan's fire had died to embers. The sky beyond the overhang was gray with patches of blue shining through. A few yards away, across the road, I saw black sand and a gray bay. A bit of sun reflected off Ari's pale hair. I wanted to draw him close, to warm his bare arms.

But I had my memories now. I knew who the dark-haired boy in the photo was. Jared and I had only started dating in the middle of the past year, but even before then, he was my best friend. He went to every one of my track meets. I went to all of his soccer games. He'd been there for me when I got the phone call about Mom. He'd always been there, whenever I'd needed him.

Until I decided to go to Iceland to find my mother,

instead of following him to study wildlife biology in San Diego. Jared and San Diego both seemed very far away now.

Even so, I wasn't Dad. I wasn't about to let Jared find out I'd gone away and forgotten him. I handed Ari his jacket. "Here. It's cold." Hadn't he almost frozen to death once already?

"I live here. I'm used to the cold." Ari drew the jacket on and looked at me. The red welts on his palms had mostly faded.

"Where's Svan?" I asked.

"He went to gather some things. For the spell, he said. We could leave now. If we get a head start, maybe he won't catch up—"

"No."

"Haley—"

I left the overhang and walked across the road. Ari followed me. The puddles were beginning to ice over, and their thin crusts crunched beneath my feet. That made no sense—it'd been summer when we left Thingvellir. Not that I could even feel the cold. I unzipped my jacket; the wind brushed my ears and bare neck. "Ari, where are we?"

Ari shrugged uneasily. "I'm not sure. Somewhere in Iceland, I think."

I glanced at the hills with their red and orange mosses. Autumn colors, though we didn't get them in Tucson. "How long have we been gone?"

"I don't know." Wind tugged at Ari's hair. "If we're lucky three, maybe four months?"

From above the hills the sun cast long shadows toward the bay. In Iceland the sun didn't set in summer, either, not for long. "And if we're not lucky?"

Ari jammed his hands into his pockets. "I've been trying not to think about that."

Thorvald has been dead many years. Warm as I was, I shivered. Muninn said time was fluid in his cave. What did that *mean*? How long had Dad been waiting for me? I scowled and dug my sneaker into the sand. Dad could wait forever, for all that I cared.

A gull flew low over the water. Behind it I saw two smaller birds, white-and-black arctic terns. If it wasn't summer, shouldn't they have migrated south? All three birds quickly flew on. "Do you know that ever since I met Hallgerd, all I dream about is fire?" I looked at the water, not Ari, as I spoke. "And about going up in flames?"

"So you want to cast a spell that could speed things along? No offense, Haley, but that doesn't seem very smart."

The worst part of the dream hadn't been the burning, though. It had been knowing that when I fell to earth, the world would burn with me. Svan's spell might take care of Hallgerd's fire, but what about mine?

Ari shook his hair out of his eyes. "We could bring the coin to Hlidarendi with my mom, like she wanted. We don't have to destroy it."

"No!" My voice came out too loud. I didn't want to even look at Katrin again.

"Haley. I'm angry with them, too, and believe me, I know all about doing stupid things because you're angry. But this—"

"You were right to tell me about my dad and your mom. That wasn't stupid."

"Oh yeah, because if I hadn't told you, you might never have run and climbed the rocks and fallen. I was so right to make that happen. To get us into this mess."

"You didn't make this mess. *She* did." Not Katrin. Hallgerd. Ari's mom and my dad had made it worse, though.

Ari kicked the damp sand. "I'd just like to see us both get out of it alive. Call me selfish, but I'd rather not have to explain to your father that Hallgerd's spell consumed you, too."

"About time this spell hurt someone besides me."

"Haley!" Ari's jaw fell open. It was several heartbeats before he spoke. "You don't mean that."

My stomach clenched. Why did I still care how Dad felt?

"Your dad was a wreck when your mom disappeared. You know that, don't you?"

The awful thing was, I did know. I'd seen how lost Dad looked when he came off that plane last summer—how lost he'd looked all this past year. "Why'd he mess around, then?"

"I don't know."

"Why the hell did he talk about getting a divorce?"

"I don't *know*. Maybe your dad and my mom both just screwed up. Maybe that's how people are."

"That's no excuse."

"I know." Ari reached for my hand. I drew mine away. He muttered something that might have been "sorry"—about Dad or about holding my hand, I couldn't tell. "Svan's part of the same saga as Hallgerd, you know. We study *Njal's Saga* next year in school, but of course Mom made me read it early. The sorcerer caused all sorts of trouble. It's not like he can be trusted."

As if I didn't know that. Ari wasn't the one Svan had tried to claim as a gift. The sun touched the hills behind us, turning the mosses to gold. Ari drew his arms around himself—was the air getting colder? In the distance, I saw Svan heading toward us along the beach, his staff in one hand, a second, smaller leather bag slung over his shoulder atop the first one. He whistled as he walked.

"Well. You two took your time waking up," the sorcerer said as he drew near. The smaller sack was wriggling. *What on earth?*

"For the spell," Svan said at my puzzled look.

"What do you mean, for the spell?" From inside the bag I heard a squeal.

Svan stared at me like I was a puzzle he was trying to figure out. "Does my kinswoman truly know so little of sorcery? We must go through all the steps of Hallgerd's spell if we wish to break it, only differently. And if Hallgerd used the spell that I believe she did, it required the blood of a white fox."

"You have a *fox* in there?" I felt sick and angry at once. *Freki,* I thought, but of course it wouldn't be him. We'd left Freki back in the mountain. *Some other fox, then.* That wasn't any better.

Nothing's as important as hurting Hallgerd, I thought. "How much blood?" I asked.

Svan seemed startled by the question. "All of it."

"Wait—you're going to *kill* it?"

"Of course not," Svan said. "You are."

"No," I said. Ari moved closer to my side, nodding his agreement.

"I don't think you understand," Svan said. "This is no small spell Hallgerd cast. If I'm reading the runes on that coin right, my niece intended to send her spirit—and yours—through time. She offered gifts to the fire realm to do so. So great a spell cannot be broken by a few drops of blood or a handful of pretty words. The breaking requires as much power as the casting. That power will be strongest if the spell is cast by Hallgerd's target. By you."

I shook my head. "There has to be another way."

"Of course. Human blood works as well. Would you prefer that?" Svan's face turned unreadable. I couldn't tell whether he meant it or not. A nose tried to push through the bag.

My stomach churned. I wanted to work with animals one day. How could I kill one?

"Mom," I whispered. *Hallgerd killed her. Hallgerd* has *to pay.*

The fox squealed once more. "You're hurting it," I said.

"Indeed. It is time to end the creature's suffering." Svan set his staff aside and handed the larger bag to me. "There's a knife inside, and a driftwood bowl to hold the blood. Take them. I will teach you all you need to do."

Svan reached into the smaller bag and pulled the fox out by its legs, which were bound together with a length of rough rope. The fox was smaller than Freki, little more than a pup, more gray than white. She writhed in Svan's hold, then looked at me, just for a moment. Her eyes rolled back in her head, but she kept struggling.

I wanted to throw up. I thought of Freki, lapping at the mead I'd offered him, following me through the tunnels, digging his claws into my shoulders to give warnings even though he wasn't supposed to interfere. Offering his companionship when I was completely alone, without even my own memories for company.

I thought of Mom in her vet clinic, patiently setting an injured dog's leg, giving a trembling cat its shots. The clinic was the one place where Mom never yelled.

I'd watched Mom put pets to sleep, too. I wasn't stupid. I knew not every animal could be saved. Sometimes there was no choice.

"Haley," Svan said, "it is only a fox." He glanced at Ari. "Surely even you know that, Ari, Katrin's son. Tell her. Only a woman—a *girl*—would be so sentimental."

"Actually, I'm rather fond of foxes," Ari said, his voice flat.

"What is this small life against the fate of the world?" Svan asked.

I reached out to stroke the fox. Her teeth snapped at my fingers. She wasn't wholly helpless, even now.

The sun was very low, its orange glow casting just a few rays of light on the water. The hills were turning to shadow. Soon it would be too dark to see.

Mom. I reached into the bag, knowing what I had to do. My hands shook as I drew out a wooden bowl the size of a cereal bowl. I set it down, then drew out a knife with a smooth bone handle, its blade encased in a leather sheath.

"No," Ari said.

I unsheathed the knife. Svan looked at Ari. "Hold the bowl," the sorcerer said.

Ari shook his head. He looked as angry as he had back at Thingvellir. "I'll have no part of this. Haley—"

Svan laughed derisively. "Haley, at least, does not lack courage." Svan knelt in front of the bowl. He took the fox's head in his hands, bracing the body between his arms. The fox went limp. Svan pulled back her head, exposing her neck.

"Be quick," Svan said. "If you're quick, there will be less pain."

Ari scowled. I knelt in front of Svan, knife clutched tightly, and leaned forward.

I sliced through the fox's bonds so fast that, for a moment, Svan didn't notice. In that instant I dropped the knife and threw myself at the sorcerer, knocking him off balance. We tumbled to the sand. The fox slashed at my sleeve, then leaped away and bounded across the beach. Ari let out a breath.

I thought of Mom bringing home one stray cat after another. My eyes stung. Mom would never have wanted me to kill an animal. Not to avenge her, not even to save her life. I'd wanted to, though. Some part of me had wanted to.

"You stupid girl!" Svan grabbed my arms and hauled me to my feet. "You're more of a fool than *she* was. This is no mere game—the very land beneath our feet is at stake!"

I fought, but the sorcerer was too strong. His fingers pressed into my shoulders, bruising me, hurting me. Ari ran at him. Svan shoved him away with one hand, then grabbed me more firmly. Ari fell dazed to the ground as Svan began shaking me, dragging me down the beach. I fought harder. Anger and fear rose in me, and the fire in me rose with it, coals bursting into flame. A wind blew, carrying the scent of hot ash. Svan howled, and I knew my fire was burning him, but he didn't let go. I tried to kick him instead. The ground gave a sharp lurch, knocking us both off our feet.

I wriggled out from under the sorcerer. The ground shook harder, and I heard tumbling rock.

I thought of water thrown over a campfire, of red embers sizzling to gray. The fire in me flickered down to a few sparks. The ground's shaking slowed, then stopped. Svan stumbled to his feet. I stepped back from him, gauging whether I could run before he grabbed me again. In the distance Ari stood, too, and ran toward us. The last rays of sun disappeared behind the hills.

Ari's jacket turned to liquid and began to flow. My breath caught. The change was much faster than before—Ari didn't stop, didn't fall to his knees. In moments he turned into a huge white bear, loping on all fours.

A bear that roared and kept running, right at Svan.

∼ *Chapter 10* ∼

Even as the bear began to leap, Svan pointed at Ari and chanted:

> *May you shed this form and show*
> *Your true self.*
> *I will fear no bear-kin!*

Fur and bearskin melted away. It was a human boy who knocked Svan to the ground and landed crouched on top of him. Sweat streamed down Ari's face. "Leave her alone."

Svan chuckled. "So you're a berserk, are you? I under-estimated you, boy." The sorcerer got to his feet, dumping Ari roughly to the ground. Ari scrambled up, shoulders tensed. I hurried to his side. His legs wobbled, and he grabbed my arm for balance.

"That's the thing about the berserks," Svan said. "You're strong enough during a change, but not much use afterward. Even so"—he grinned, as if he hadn't attacked me a moment before—"you could do worse, Haley."

Ari and I took a few steps back. "Just stay away," I said.

Svan held out his hands as if to say, *Whatever.* His palms were burned and beginning to blister. He hardly seemed to notice. *I did that.* The thought didn't bother me as much as it should have.

Svan looked at Ari. "So whose line are you through? Skallagrim, perhaps?"

Ari eyed him warily. "Mom and I are through Hallgerd's line, actually, just like Haley."

"Indeed?" Svan stroked his beard. "What of your father's people?"

Ari drew his arms across his chest. "My father has nothing to do with anything. He ran away before I was born." Yet he glanced at his jacket, as if uncertain.

Svan reached toward the jacket. Ari growled at him, and Svan stepped back. *Score one for us.*

"My dad left it behind." Ari switched to English—words for me, not Svan. His wary gaze never left the sorcerer, though. "I found the jacket in Mom's closet a few years ago. I do not know why she didn't get rid of it. I do not know why he didn't take it with him."

"Do you think he knew? About being a bear?" I spoke English, too, while Svan stared at us both.

"How should I know?" Ari snapped. "It is not like he ever calls."

Wind tugged at my sleeves, my strange short hair. "I'm sorry." I tried to imagine never having known my dad. Angry as I was, the thought brought no comfort.

Ari shifted uneasily. "He is the one who should be sorry, yeah?" Silence thickened around us, no sound but the wind.

"So," Svan said, "if you two are done with your love talk, perhaps we can get back to business?" Tension crept into his casual words. "You felt the earthquake, Haley. That was Hallgerd's work, of course." He glanced down at his burned hands. "I did not know Hallgerd's magic had rooted in you so deeply."

Svan didn't know the fire in me hadn't come from Hallgerd. The coin remained in my pocket, but its power seemed a small thing beside the fire banked beneath my skin. Would Svan decide he needed to destroy me, too, if he knew I held fire of my own?

Was it really my fire that had caused the earth to shake? *Wouldn't Dad love that? Earthquakes whenever he wants them.* I fought down a hysterical giggle.

"The earthquakes will only get worse, the longer the coin remains intact," Svan said. "If you will not destroy it, give it to me. The spell will be weaker if I cast it, but at least I don't lack the will to do what needs to be done." Svan stepped toward me. Ari tensed at my side. The sorcerer held out his hand.

The sky and clouds were dark now, the world around us mostly shadow. I looked toward the overhang. A huge boulder had slid down from the hill above it, half blocking the opening. In the distance, other piles of rubble lay at the base of other hills, sent tumbling down by the quake.

People *died* in earthquakes. Had Muninn been right to hide me away, where I couldn't do any harm? But Muninn couldn't have known what would happen, not unless the raven could see the future as well as remember the past.

If I gave the coin to Svan, it wouldn't do anything for my fire, and Svan would find another fox to kill. I couldn't let him do that.

Not even to save the world from Hallgerd's magic, which I already knew could do as much harm as mine? *Mom*— Just thinking about Mom opened up a huge empty space inside of me. The sparks within me yearned toward that place. Offered to fill it, to burn the ache away.

No. I forced the sparks down.

"The coin, Haley." Svan's gray eyes were hard as stone.

"What if we send the coin back to Hallgerd?" What if we did what Katrin wanted? Thinking about Katrin made me want to dig my nails into my palms—but better that than hurting one of Freki's kin.

"Don't be stupid," Svan said. "Hallgerd would only gain more power were the coin returned to her. Only your holding it keeps the spell in check, and even that protection will only last so long. There is no telling what Hallgerd will do once her own power is set free. She was very angry when last I saw her."

How long ago was that, though? *I'm content to live and die by Gunnar's side.* Maybe Hallgerd wouldn't do anything after all.

Or maybe she would. I drew my arms around myself. It was nearly full dark now. Through the thinning clouds, a huge yellow moon rose over the water. I still didn't want to give anything back to Hallgerd, but this wasn't just about what I wanted.

Svan stepped toward me. Ari stepped toward him, teeth bared.

"Stop!" I told them both. "I—I need to think!"

Svan halted. "I need to get my courage up," I said, thinking fast. Ari returned to my side. Fire or no fire, neither of us was stronger than Svan. That meant we had to delay him and get away—but how? The knife lay a few yards behind us, by the bowl. I wasn't sure I could get to it faster than Svan could. All I had in my backpack were some chocolate malt balls, a bottle of water, and—a skin of mead. Mead that wasn't drugged, but that was too strong for mortals to handle.

"Let's have a drink," I said—too quickly, but Svan didn't seem to notice. "To help with that courage."

Ari gave me a puzzled look, but the hardness left

Svan's eyes. "You did not say you had drink with you, Haley. The world can wait a short time more. Where is this drink?"

"In my pack." I glanced at the overhang, lit by moonlight, half-covered by the boulder. I knew it wasn't safe to go into buildings after earthquakes. Was a rocky outcrop any different?

Svan didn't seem concerned—he grinned and headed for the overhang, his feet crunching through half-frozen puddles. As he dove beneath the stones, Ari whispered in English, "Do you really think that is wise?"

"Trust me," I said, also in English. *This had better work,* I thought.

Svan returned and handed me the pack, which was still a little damp. He'd brought the last few pieces of driftwood as well, and he set them down on the beach. He slid a few pieces of papery wood beneath them, made a motion with his hands, and whispered words I couldn't hear. A small flame caught beneath the wood. The fire in me rose in response.

With a whoosh the wood burst into brighter flame. I burst into flame, too, into fire reaching for the sky, even as the earth shook beneath me—

No! With a wrench I forced the flames down, down, down. I staggered back, sweat pouring down my face, knowing that I hadn't really been burning, not on the outside. Svan's fire kept going, not so brightly now. The earth was still. Ari caught me as I fell to my knees. "Sorry," I whispered.

Svan gave me a long look. "This had better be strong drink."

"It is. I promise." I got to my feet, rummaged through the bag, and pulled out Freki's wineskin. I pulled out the malt balls, too, inhaled a mouthful, and offered the bag to Ari, who did the same. Somehow we'd have to get real food eventually. I sat cross-legged beside Svan and handed him the mead.

Ari offered Svan the malt balls as well—less than a handful was left—as he sat beside me. The sorcerer shook his head and uncorked the skin. *Please, please let this work.*

Svan drew the skin toward his lips, stopped, and sniffed it. His eyes narrowed. *Shit.*

"What treachery is this?" Svan's voice was low, like Dad's voice when he got angry. "Do you think me a fool, who does not know what you offer me?"

"Umm." *Now what?*

Ari looked back and forth between us. "The mead of poetry," Svan said, answering his unasked question. "Haven't I rested in Muninn's mountain long enough, Haley?" Svan's voice dripped disdain as he handed the skin back to me, still open.

"Wait—that's the mead of poetry?" Ari's eyes grew wide by the firelight. He reached toward the skin.

"Don't." I drew it away. "It'll make you sleep—"

"Yeah, but—"

"But *what?*"

"If I could write a decent poem for once—a decent song . . ." He reached for the skin again, then hesitated.

"Oh no, you don't!" I pulled the thing out of his reach. "I *need* you here." I turned the skin upside down. No way was I taking a chance on Ari going unconscious on me.

The mead steamed as it hit the sand. The wind died, all at once.

Svan grabbed the skin from my hands and righted it. The remaining liquid sloshed inside. "You *are* a fool," he muttered.

The earth trembled, ever-so-slightly, less like an earthquake than someone shivering at a too-gentle touch. Svan gestured down the beach. A fog bank moved toward us, silver gray in the moonlight. Within that fog a man ambled toward us with a slow rolling gait. His broad-brimmed hat covered one eye; his cloak was the same color as the fog.

Do not spill that. My master would not like it. How stupid *was* I? I hadn't thought about Freki's warning, though. I'd thought only about Ari.

Yet the man didn't seem angry. He didn't seem in any hurry to reach us, either. He smiled as he made his way down the beach. Then he saw me watching him, and he winked, though I should have been too far away to see. The trembling of the earth moved down beneath my skin. I started shivering and couldn't stop. I looked at Ari and saw that he trembled, too, even as he cursed slowly and steadily under his breath.

My sight blurred, and I saw only fog, but the shivering went on. The fire in me burned hot, hot, hot, even as I shivered.

Svan corked the mead and tossed it into my backpack. "You must go." He began putting other things in the pack as well: the wooden bowl, the knife in its sheath.

Leaving sounded awfully good to me, only— "Wait, if that's Freki and Muninn's master, can't *he* destroy the coin?" Destroy it without killing anything in the process?

"Haley." Svan spoke slowly, as if to a small child. "Muninn's master does not fear the end of the world. He will fight it, to be sure—he and the fire spirits are old enemies— but he will throw everything he has into that fighting. You hesitate to kill a single fox; to him we're all less than foxes. He won't hesitate to sacrifice us."

I opened my mouth; no sound came out. Ari got to his feet, reached for my hand, and pulled me up as well.

The mead had soaked deep into the sand, but steam still rose from the spot. Svan dug a couple of other items out of his bag—a raven's claw, a dull black stone—and tossed them into the backpack as well.

"I don't need that stuff. I—"

Svan reached for my shoulder, thought better of it, and let his hand drop. His expression turned almost gentle. "You are my kinswoman. I will do what I can to protect you. I will hold him off as long as I can. Only you must make it worth it. Destroy the coin. Not only for the land's sake. I felt the fire within you—Hallgerd's spell could consume you, too, if you do not end it."

My fire didn't come from Hallgerd's spell, but even now I didn't say so. "What about you?" What did I care about him, after the way he'd attacked me?

A sly smile crossed the sorcerer's face. "I may be an old man, but I have a few tricks left in me." He cast a wry look Ari's way. "Perhaps I'll see if my poems have more worth than yours. If nothing else, it should make a good story."

The fog was closer now. I heard footsteps crunching over the sand. Svan thrust the bag at me and I zipped it shut. "Thank you."

"Go!" the sorcerer said. He grabbed his staff and walked toward the fog. "Hello there!" he called, as if greeting an old friend.

Ari looked at me. "Now we run?" he said.

"No." I remembered Katrin's words. *You must never run from magic.*

So we walked away this time, even as Svan disappeared into the fog behind us.

∽ *Chapter 11* ∽

We followed the dirt road, while the earth stilled and our shivering eased. When I glanced back, I saw only fog, no sign of either Svan or Freki's master. The fog disappeared into the distance as we walked on. The moon cast a bright path over the water to our left. To our right, boulders and jumbled rocks lay at the base of the dark hills.

A sudden roar made me jump. Ari and I scrambled off the road as bright lights blinded us. I backed toward the hills, knowing there was nowhere to hide—

A truck rumbled by, tires crunching over the gravel. Ari let out a nervous laugh. I laughed, too, though my legs felt like rubber. I'd forgotten there were cars. Did I think the entire world had disappeared when Muninn spirited me away?

Ari stopped laughing and ran into the road, chasing the truck and calling after the driver. It was some sort of emergency vehicle, blue lights silently flashing. The driver didn't even slow down, and the truck quickly disappeared out of sight. "Ah, well," Ari said as I caught up with him. "So much for our ride."

"The man in the fog," I said, because suddenly it seemed safe to talk again. "Who *was* he?" Aside from being someone who I knew, down to my bones, that I didn't want to anger.

Ari looked uneasily back the way we'd come. "I'm not sure I should name him. Just in case that would—you know—attract his attention. Look him up when we get back. A one-eyed man with a floppy hat. Before this all happened, I'd have told you he wasn't real, either." Ari hesitated. "Speaking of getting back, where are we going, Haley?"

I swallowed hard. "To your mom." I still didn't want to go to Katrin, but even though Svan had bought us some time, no way was I casting his spell. "I'll give your mom the coin. She can send it back to Hallgerd, like she wanted to before I ran."

Ari nodded. The gravel crunched beneath our feet. He reached into his jacket and fished something out from an inner pocket. A cell phone.

"Wait—you have a phone?" I stared as Ari powered it up. The phone's white light seemed as unnatural as the rumbling truck.

"I tried to call out while you were sleeping. Couldn't get a signal." Ari frowned at the display. "We're still out of range. I'll keep trying. If we can figure out where we are, Mom can pick us up."

Whatever happens, you can always call me. I hoped Katrin meant that, because right now we didn't have much choice. I looked at the phone display over Ari's shoulder. Once we got a signal, we'd know the time—the year. I felt a chill that had nothing to do with the cold.

Ari powered down the phone. The wind started back up, but the coals deep inside me kept me warm.

Ari shivered, though. "I'm sorry about your mom," he said.

"Yeah, me too." We walked around a patch of slick ice that shone beneath the bright moon.

"Also, I'm sorry I was an idiot about the mead," Ari said.

"I think that one's more my fault than yours." For all I knew, Ari wouldn't really have drunk it. He'd only said he was thinking about it.

Ari glanced back the way we'd come. "There are more important things than writing good poems." He gave a wry smile. "I should know."

"Hey, I *liked* your poem!"

Ari laughed. "It's good that someone does."

"No, really. I think it's cool you write poetry." I'd never been much of a writer. Staring at a blank page or a blank screen made me feel restless, like I should ditch the computer and go for a run instead.

Ari shrugged. "They're more like songs than poems, anyway. And like the sorcerer said—they're not very good."

"You're going to take *his* word for it?"

"No, here, I'll show you." Ari pulled a small notebook—the notebook he'd had at Thingvellir—from his back jeans pocket and handed it to me, along with his flashlight. He watched nervously as I opened it.

The pages were swollen and brittle, the words smudged with water. I realized it didn't matter. I stared at the writing by the blue LED light, trying to make sense of it. "I can't read Icelandic. I can only speak it." I tried to keep the frustration out of my voice. *Getting to speak a whole new language is pretty cool by itself.* But I wanted to read Ari's poetry.

"Heh. I bet no one was writing yet when that mead was brewed. I'm spared from you reading my terrible words, then." Ari took the notebook back.

"I bet you're good," I said.

Ari tried to smooth down the pages, gave up, and shoved the notebook back into his pocket. "You'll lose all your money making bets like that."

"No, I mean it. Can you sing something for me?"

"When we get home. I'll sing—and play—for you then."

"You play, too?"

"Keyboard, mostly." He brushed his pale bangs out of

his face, looking uncomfortable. "Did you mean what you said? About needing me here?"

"Yeah." A rockslide blocked the road. We walked on the sand to get around it. "But—I don't know if I meant it like that."

Ari nodded, as if he'd expected as much. That made me angry for some reason. "I don't know that I *didn't* mean it like that, either," I snapped. "I just don't know. You know?"

"Yeah," Ari said, as if that had actually made sense.

I drew my arms around myself. "All I know is that we have to deal with that coin. After that . . ." My fingers dug for my palms. I forced them away. *How am I supposed to go home without Mom? I can't do this.* "I don't know what happens after that. Okay?"

Ari nodded again, more slowly. "I'll try not to be an idiot about that, too." He stopped and looked into the distance.

"What are you thinking?" I asked him.

Ari smiled for real. "I'm thinking that looks like a farmhouse on that hill, and that maybe they'll let us use their phone."

Bits of jagged glass littered the ground around the house— all the windows were broken, and an entire wall was missing in the back, turned to a pile of concrete rubble and leaving a kitchen filled with broken dishes open to the wind. My throat went dry. Had I really caused the quake with the fire in me? I reached down and touched a piece of broken glass. It pierced my finger, and blood flowed from the wound.

Blood and a thin wisp of smoke. I pressed my finger swiftly to my mouth, fire receding as I focused on the pain. *My blood couldn't have been burning. . . .* I drew my finger free. There was no smoke now, just a pinprick cut that had already stopped bleeding.

There was a tent set up in the backyard, but no one answered from it when we called. "Maybe they left to stay with family." Ari turned back toward the broken wall. "You think we can find a phone in there?" He set a foot on the pile of rubble.

I grabbed his arm. "That really would be stupid." A metal roof arched over the spot where the wall had been. Who knew when it might fall in?

"Just trying to do something useful for once." Ari stepped back. "Doesn't matter. Phone's probably dead, anyway."

We ate the last of the malt balls and drank the last of the water as we walked on. My stomach rumbled. At least water wasn't a problem. We refilled the bottle when we passed a stream that trickled down the hillside, after Ari said it was safe to drink.

The road turned to thick mud that coated my sneakers. The clouds cleared, leaving behind a sky full of stars, the white band of the Milky Way burning across them, visible even with the moon.

The mud began to freeze, slush crunching beneath our feet. The moon set, and the stars faded. Color slowly returned to the world, revealing bright yellow and orange grasses clinging to hillsides dusted with frost. The road veered away from the water, and the sun rose behind us. The frost glittered like diamonds, bright as the stars had been. I caught my breath. "Beautiful," I whispered.

Ari smiled a little. "I'll show you something more beautiful." He pointed into the distance. Sun glinted off the windows of a long white building. "Maybe someone will be home this time."

As we got closer, we saw people outside. We hurried up the building's low gravel drive. "You have to understand," a man was saying in English, "that it is very unusual to have earthquakes in the Westfjords. I don't know how long it will take to get the all-clear to go back inside. We have no injuries, so we're not a priority."

"The Westfjords." Ari nodded, as if he knew where we were. "That's not so far."

The building—Hotel Laugarholl, the bright red words painted on it said—didn't seem damaged, even with its large windows. Maybe it hadn't been a very large quake—or maybe the hotel got lucky, the way houses did in wildfires, when the flames spared some homes but not others. A half dozen people stood around in pajamas and jackets on the building's yellow lawn. A few rumpled blankets lay on the ground. In spite of not being cleared to go inside, a couple of men were bringing out food and piling it onto a table.

Ari walked up to one of the men. "Excuse me, could we borrow your phone?" he asked in Icelandic. The man didn't look at him, just set down a tray of sliced meat and headed back toward the door. Ari followed, repeating the question in English, but the man didn't turn around.

Two women in jackets and jeans headed for the table, talking quietly in what sounded like German. Ari followed them. *"Guten Tag, haben Sie ein Handy?"* His German was more hesitant than his English. The women walked right by, as if they didn't see him.

An uneasy feeling crawled down my spine. I thought of how that emergency vehicle had driven right past us. Of how no one had answered by the farmhouse we'd stopped at.

The other guests—two older couples—got into line behind the Germans. They were debating in English whether to still go on a hike they'd planned. I tapped one of the women on the shoulder. She drew her arms around herself but didn't turn around.

Ari stepped right in front of a man carrying a couple of pitchers. The man kept walking, stumbling as he bumped into Ari. Thick milk sloshed over one of the pitchers. The man cursed himself for his clumsiness as Ari stepped out of his way.

They couldn't see us. They really couldn't. Just like—

A cloud drifted past the sun. Ari returned to my side.

"'None shall remember you, beyond these stones.'" My voice sounded unnaturally loud. "'None shall see you, comfort you, aid you. I leave you alone, alone, alone.'"

Ari's eyes went wide. "We are like ghosts to them."

"That's impossible." Even more impossible than everything else that had happened since I came to Iceland.

Ari began cursing in English and Icelandic both. I stared at the people piling food onto their plates. I didn't feel like a ghost. How could anyone make the entire world forget us?

Ari stopped cursing and laughed a little. "At least if we do anything stupid now," he said in Icelandic, "no one will know, right?"

In the distance, a gull cried out. Even if we made it back to Dad and Katrin, what if they couldn't see us, either? What if they couldn't *remember* us? What if no one could, not Jared or any of my friends at school or my grandparents or cousins? Panic rose in me. It made no difference how long we'd been gone if no one remembered us—knew us. "What are we supposed to do now?"

Ari shrugged uneasily. "Eat breakfast? I don't know about you, but I'm starving. And, well, we should eat while we can."

I forced the panic down. Sweat beaded on my skin. My stomach rumbled, louder than before. When had I last had anything but stale jerky and chocolate malt balls? "Can ghosts even eat?" I followed Ari as he got into line behind the hikers.

Ari lifted a slice of meat off the table and tasted it. "Yeah. They can." He grabbed a plate and bowl and piled them high.

So did I. I wondered if the dishes looked to everyone else like they were flying through the air or if maybe they disappeared when we touched them—but when I glanced around to see how people were reacting, they all just happened to be looking in other directions.

The guests found spots to eat on the blankets on the ground. So did we. "Like a picnic, yeah?" Ari said.

"A freaky little invisible earthquake picnic, sure." I tried to laugh, but my throat tightened around the sound. *I'm not panicking. I am* not *panicking.* I sat down by Ari's side, balancing my plate in my lap.

One of the hikers spread a newspaper out beside him. I still couldn't read the Icelandic, but apparently *19 September* was the same as in English—and the year was our year. I let out a breath and pointed. "We've only been gone three months," I said. *More time has passed for Hallgerd than for us.*

Ari nodded slowly, and his shoulders relaxed a little. "That's something, at least." He dove into his food.

I forced a slice of cold lamb past my lips. It tasted amazing—once I began eating, I couldn't stop. I devoured the lamb, a couple of hardboiled eggs, several slices of bread with some kind of pâté, and even something I'd thought was yogurt but turned out to be more of the awful sour milk I'd had at the guesthouse.

We filled my backpack with more food: granola and hardboiled eggs, cheese and more lamb. I began to feel guilty—I reached into my wallet, pulled out the bills inside, and left them on the table, wedged beneath a serving platter. I had no idea whether that covered all the food we'd taken—or if anyone could even see my money—but it would have to do.

The German tourists pulled out a map. Ari looked over their shoulders. "I know where we are," he said. "Strandir, on the coast—near Bear's Fjord." He gave a wry laugh. "I should feel right at home. Though I bet they just named it for Svan's father, Bjorn. I think Svan lived around here."

"How far are we from Reykjavik?" I asked. The tourists didn't look up as we spoke.

"Two hundred, two hundred fifty kilometers south?"

I did the math in my head: maybe a hundred and fifty miles. *Way too far to walk.* "Maybe there's a phone inside. We can call your mom from there."

Ari nodded. Neither of us mentioned that the building wasn't cleared as safe to enter, or that we weren't sure Katrin would be able to hear us when we called. You couldn't just forget your own kid, could you?

The wooden doors were propped open. Inside, the

reception desk was buried in books and postcards and
tourist brochures that must have fallen from the shelves
behind it. Ari dug a phone out from beneath them,
brought it to his ear, and frowned. "Right," he said. "On
the map, there were some towns. Holmavik is about
twenty kilometers away. I think that's our best chance for
a signal."

I nodded. That wasn't so bad—I could run twelve miles,
if I had to. I followed Ari away from the hotel. The frozen
slush was melting, turning the dirt road back to mud. I felt
for the coin in my pocket. The coals inside me warmed at
its touch. Did the ground tremble slightly? The trembling
stopped when I drew my hand away.

I'd get the coin to Katrin. With any luck—if Katrin was
right, if Svan and Muninn were wrong—the land would be
safe from Hallgerd's spell after that. As for the fire in me,
well, maybe Katrin would know what to do about that, too.

The few clouds burned away, leaving behind a deep
blue sky that reminded me of Tucson, except the sun was
too low, its light too thin. A breeze caressed my neck. I
thought of the hot desert winds at home, like a dragon's
breath against my skin in summer.

The coals in me sparked hot at the thought. The ground
shuddered beneath my feet. *"I can give you fire."* Not Hallgerd's voice this time—the rough voice I'd heard in the fire
realm. I unzipped my jacket and threw my arms open to the
wind. *Cold. I like the cold.* A lie—I hated the chilly winter

mornings back home—but the fire in me turned merely warm again.

"You okay, Haley?" Ari reached for my hand. His palm felt cool. I wrapped my fingers around his, as if I could soak up the cold if only I held on hard enough.

With his free hand Ari fished his cell phone out of his pocket and powered it up. "Hey, we have a signal!" His grip on my hand tightened. "Oh, look, I have four hundred eighteen text messages. I'll check them later." He dialed one-handed.

"Hello, Mom?" Ari's voice was strained—he was angry at his mom, too, after all. "Hello?"

He pressed redial. "Mom? Can you hear me?" Ari fell silent. Very quietly, he shut the phone and put it back into his pocket.

"Dropped call?" I asked, but I knew better.

"No." Ari swallowed hard, cursed softly. "She couldn't hear me. The people at the hotel, they weren't so bad—they don't know us. But Mom . . ." His voice tightened.

Katrin couldn't help us. I stared down at our linked hands. No one could. "We're on our own."

"Maybe Mom will see the number. Then she'll at least know we're all right. I should try a text message." Ari's voice was bleak, though, and I knew he didn't expect that to work, either.

Alone, alone, alone. I clutched Ari's hand so tightly my knuckles turned white. Did Dad even remember who I was?

What had he thought when I ran away and didn't come back? The coin felt warm through my pocket. *It* wasn't going to disappear just because Ari and I had turned to ghosts.

If the spell lands on you, you must cast it back again. Thorgerd, Hallgerd's daughter, had said that in her spellbook. *The means of the casting, plus other useful spells, follow.*

"I think"—I drew a breath—"I think it's up to me now. Your mom gave me a copy of her spellbook."

"I know." Ari stared down at our linked fingers. We reached an intersection with another dirt road, one with less mud. He turned right. "She stayed up half the night translating that thing."

I pictured Katrin copying spell after spell that she thought might protect me. My stomach felt funny. "Your mom said to take the coin to Hlidarendi."

"Gunnar and Hallgerd's home, yeah. It's maybe another hundred kilometers east of Reykjavik."

"So two hundred miles total. Maybe a little more."

"Pretty long walk," Ari agreed.

"You don't have to come." I'd been assuming he would, but maybe that wasn't fair. He'd already gotten into enough trouble trying to rescue me. Yet the thought of going on without him made me feel funny, too.

"Like there's anyone else I can talk to?" Ari laughed, then stopped abruptly. "You're serious, aren't you? Don't be stupid, Haley—of course I'm coming with you. We're in this together."

I squeezed his hand, taking comfort from the thought. No one else could hear us, but at least we could hear each other.

Ari smiled. "Maybe there's a bus we can catch in Holmavik. I'm sure they won't mind a couple of invisible passengers, yeah?"

"Yeah." *We can do this. Send the coin back, and figure out everything else after that.* We kept walking, still holding hands.

The wind died down. A sudden burst of tinny music made me jump. It was the *Star Wars* theme, and it was coming from Ari's pocket. He fished out his phone and stared at it.

"It's ringing," Ari said. "I don't know the number—" He quickly flipped the phone open. "Hello?"

I bet it's just some telemarketer. I bet they won't hear us, either.

Ari listened a moment, and his face grew very strange. "Yes, of course," he said in English. He released my hand and offered me the phone. "It is for you, Haley. He says his name is Jared, and he says he'd like to talk to you."

∽ *Chapter 12* ∽

I grabbed the phone. *"Jared?"*

"Haley? Oh God, is it really you?"

My stomach did a little flip at the sound of Jared's voice. "Yeah, it's me." I sat down, right at the side of the road, because I suddenly didn't trust my legs to hold me up. Ari sat down beside me, keeping a careful distance.

"You can hear me," I said into the phone. Speaking English felt strange.

"Of course I can hear you. Haley, where on earth have you—" Jared's voice rose, caught. "We thought you were dead, or kidnapped, or lost in the wilderness, or—"

"Jared." He was babbling. He always babbled when he got nervous. It made me want to babble, too, to tell him everything, to talk for hours and hours until both our voices were hoarse. But I didn't know if we had hours, or when Jared might stop hearing me, too. "I'm fine. Really."

"You don't sound fine. Where are you? Have you called your dad? He gave me this number months ago, said it belonged to the guy you disappeared with. It kept going to voice mail until today—"

"We're having—a problem with the phone. Have you spoken to Dad? Is he back home? Is he okay?"

"Of course he's not okay, Haley." Jared's voice sounded like it might snap any second. "And of course he's not home. He's in Iceland, looking for you. Haley, where—"

"Do you have his number? No—wait." For all I knew Jared's call was a bit of freaky good luck that wouldn't happen again. "I need you to call him for me. Can you do that?"

"Of course, but—"

"Call him. Please. Tell him I'm all right." I drew a shaky breath. Whatever Dad had done, he deserved to know that much. "Tell him to tell Katrin that Ari and I are going to Hlidarendi. She'll know why."

"Hilda—where?"

"Hlidarendi." I did my best to spell the name. "You'll tell them?"

"Haley, what's going on?"

The worry in his voice made me want to reach through the phone and hold him. But even if I could have, he probably wouldn't have been able to see me. "Tell Dad I'm sorry

I ran. Tell him—" *That I forgive him.* I couldn't get the words out, because they weren't true. "Tell him I'm on my way home, okay?"

"Are you in some sort of trouble? Should I call the police?"

"Please, Jared."

"Okay, I'll call your dad. Right now. Just don't go anywhere. I'll call you back, I promise. Keep the phone on, all right?"

I let out a breath. "Thanks, Jared."

"God, Haley, you have no idea how good it is to hear your voice. I've missed you so much. Don't go anywhere—I'll call right back. I love you."

"Love you, too," I said, just like always when hanging up with Jared. Only after I closed the phone did I realize my hands were shaking.

Ari took the phone, his expression unreadable. He opened it and slowly dialed. "Hey, Mom?" he said in Icelandic. He waited a moment, then shook his head. "It's no good."

"Jared will call them. And then he'll call us back, if he can." I switched back to Icelandic, too.

Ari nodded slowly. "We should keep walking." He shoved the phone into his pocket and got to his feet, but he didn't reach for my hand this time. I stood as well, and we walked on in awkward silence. Around us, the hillsides were bright with autumn scrub.

The road headed uphill, then flattened out, hills giving way to barren stony flats, with gray rocks scattered about and a few dead mosses clinging to the spaces between them. The wind picked up. Ari's phone remained silent.

"It makes no sense," I said. "Why could Jared call?"

Ari shrugged. "Clearly, the power of your true love is stronger than Muninn's spell."

"Don't joke," I snapped. What did true love even mean? It had been so good to talk to Jared, but it was good to walk by Ari's side, too, awkwardness and all. How could both those things be true at once?

"Who says I'm joking?" Ari said. "You have a better explanation?"

Wind blew over the stones, making a mournful sound. I thought of Mom and Dad, and I scowled. "What makes you so sure there's any such thing as true love?"

"You'll put songwriters out of business, talking that way. Force us to find honest work." Ari managed a strained smile. "Seriously, Haley. Of course there's such a thing as true love."

I kicked a stone out of the road. "Yeah, well, tell that to my mom. Or yours, for that matter."

Ari frowned. "I didn't say there wasn't a lot of other crap that gets in the way."

"Tell it to Hallgerd's dead husbands." I bet Gunnar thought Hallgerd loved him, too, right up until she refused him those locks of her hair.

Ari gave a bitter laugh. "Yeah, well, there is that."

I thought of the voices in Muninn's mountain, of the woman whose lover ran off to Norway without her. I wondered how much true love one would find if one sifted through all the mountain's memories—all the world's memories.

Except Freki had said the mountain didn't have all the world's memories, only Iceland's. "That's why!" I said. "Muninn's magic is only for Iceland. Jared's in the States, so the spell doesn't affect him. That *has* to be it! Call someone else, Ari. Call them now."

Ari fished the phone out of his pocket and stared at it thoughtfully. "Who do you suggest I call?"

I gave him the number for Tucson's directory assistance, because I couldn't bear to hear a voice I knew and have that person not hear me in turn.

"You'll run up my bill with all these overseas calls." Ari gave a wry smile. "The country code is—one, right?" He dialed and put the phone to his ear. "Hello?" he said in English. "I would like to order a medium pepperoni and puffin pizza." He waited, then shut the phone and spoke in Icelandic. "She said I was very funny. The operator."

I let out a long breath. "Muninn's wrong. We're not forgotten by everyone."

"No," Ari said. "Only by everyone I know except you and some friends on the Internet."

"Oh." *Of course.* I could go back to the States, to Jared

and my grandparents and my other friends at school, but what about Ari? There was no *only Iceland* for him—this was his home. "Maybe you could call your mom from the U.S. Maybe she'd hear you from there. We could take the coin away with us." Would *that* end Hallgerd's spell, and douse my own fire as well? Maybe all we needed to do was leave, and everything would be okay. "We could sneak onto a plane. No one would see us."

"Not until we land." Ari's steps crunched over the dirt road. "How would you explain me to U.S. Customs?"

"Well, you'd have to get a passport, but—"

"I have a passport." Ari looked down at his hands. "How would you explain if I'm not human when we land? What do you think an angry polar bear would do to an airplane, anyway?" He laughed uneasily. "Bear on a plane. It's like a movie."

Images of the bears in national parks, tearing the roofs off cars to get at coolers, flashed through my head. We didn't even know what made Ari change into a bear. Was it when he got angry, like with Svan? Anger seemed to feed the fire in me as well. "Maybe the bear spell will end, too, if we leave. We should call Jared, anyway. Let him know what's going on." *Jared should have called us back by now.*

Ari handed me the phone. I dialed, but it went straight to voice mail. *Maybe Jared's battery died. Or maybe he's still talking to Dad.*

We reached another road, right at the edge of a deep

blue fjord. Fog hung over the water, though the sky above was clear. We turned right again, following the fjord inland. The fog thickened.

"So your boyfriend," Ari asked abruptly. "What's he like?"

"He's—" I hadn't told Ari he was my boyfriend. Then again, you didn't exactly say "love you" to a casual acquaintance. "He's *Jared*," I said. *It's none of your business,* I thought. *Yeah, right. When you kiss someone and hold his hand and then he finds out you have a boyfriend, he's going to be just a little bit curious. People are funny that way.* "Jared and I—we've known each other forever. Since the third grade, anyway."

Ari raised a pale eyebrow. "You've had a boyfriend since the third grade?"

"No!" A flush crawled up my face. "We only started dating this year, but we've been best friends since we were little kids." Jared had always been there, just like Mom and Dad. We talked about everything. I thought of his serious brown eyes when he listened to me. I thought of the way his T-shirt clung to his sweaty skin on the soccer field, and my face grew hot. I forced my thoughts back to the road and the thickening fog. The air felt damp against my neck and face, and I could only see a few feet ahead of us now. "So, you have many girlfriends?" I asked Ari. Maybe he had someone waiting in Reykjavik for him, too, someone he couldn't call because of Muninn's spell.

"Oh sure, hundreds of girlfriends," Ari said. I looked at him, and he gave a wry laugh. "No, actually, I'm between girlfriends right now."

"How long—"

"Have I been between girlfriends?" Ari paused, as if thinking about that. "Roughly—sixteen years, yeah."

"Wait, you haven't—" *Was that his first kiss?* I glanced at him, at the way his white bangs fell into his face. I thought of the worried look in his eyes when I woke up, not remembering who he was. "I find that hard to believe," I said.

Ari seemed suddenly very interested in the road beneath his feet. "The girls I've asked out didn't share your point of view." He shrugged uncomfortably, but then a smile tugged at the corner of his mouth. "Hey, you can't write good songs if you don't get your heart broken, right?"

I managed a laugh. I'd known Jared forever, but right then I wanted nothing as much as to reach for Ari's hand again.

Was that what had happened with Dad and Katrin? A stray thought—only Dad had followed where it led? That was different, though. Mom and Dad were *married.* Still, I kept my hands to myself.

Farmhouses disappeared into the mist. A row of sheep slowly crossed the road ahead of us, little more than shadows, the fog giving them a strange dignity. As we kept walking even Ari grew indistinct, a shadow seen through the gray. He took another step, disappeared—

"Ari!" I grabbed for his hand after all and felt his cool fingers grasping mine. He was still here. Of course he was still here. I could see him now, just barely, through the fog. I held my other hand in front of my face. I could barely see my own fingers. Tendrils of wet mist curled around us, soupy-thick. The road was barely visible, and I couldn't see the water.

"Right," Ari said. "Perhaps we should stop for a while."

We got onto the shoulder of the road, huddling down amid damp rocks and springy mosses. Water beaded on my skin and jacket and the backpack I set down beside me. Fog swirled around us, coating the stones. The gray air felt clammy against my neck. Inside me the fire grew a little, keeping me warm. I reached a hand toward the fog. At my touch it sizzled and burned away, leaving a small clear area around us. Beneath us, the ground began to shake.

"Haley!"

I drew my hand into a fist, digging fingers into my palm, not quite breaking skin. The ground grew still. The fog settled back in, but the faint scent of sulfur lingered in the air. I forced my fingers apart.

Ari touched the back of my hand. "You're so warm. Ever since we jumped through the fire. The creatures there—they didn't touch me, but they touched you. Your hair—" He reached for my short hair, drew away. "What happened there?"

I drew my arms around my knees. Damp moss soaked through the seat of my jeans. "I told the fire spirits to leave you alone. They wanted some sort of payment for that, just like Muninn wanted payment for my memories. They asked for my hair, so of course I said yes, because we were both about to be burned alive." Sweat beaded on my face at the memory of that fire. "Only the fire spirits said they were giving me some of their fire in turn. They seemed to think it was a trade."

For several heartbeats Ari didn't speak. The fog made the world seem very small, just the two of us in a gray cocoon. I stared at the mist clinging to Ari's white eyelashes, wondering what it would be like to kiss him now, with all my memories intact.

"This rescuing thing—I think maybe you're better at it than me," Ari said at last. He pulled up a tuft of wet moss, examined it thoughtfully. "So we have two problems—sending the coin back to Hallgerd, and stopping you from setting off earthquakes everywhere you go."

"The coin first."

Ari nodded. "Is there anything in Mom's notebook for this?"

"I don't know. I kind of got stuck on the page about turning bears back into boys, you know?" I unzipped the pack and pulled out the notebook. The pages weren't smudged and swollen like Ari's notebook had been. Of course not—Katrin had used one of her waterproof field notebooks. The paper was a little wrinkled, nothing more, and the words were clear. She'd probably used a waterproof pen as well. She'd done all she could to make sure I wouldn't lose the words she'd translated.

I flipped past the pages I'd already read. *A spell for restoring one's own memory.* I wondered whether we could apply that to the entire island—but the spell had to be cast by the one who'd forgotten. *A spell for returning berserks to their true form.*

The spell for sending back the coin. I stopped and read that spell. There was a list of things it needed, like the ingredients in a recipe book. *A wooden bowl. A black fire stone.* (*Lignite,* Katrin called it in parentheses.) *A raven's claw.* All the things Svan had given me, only he'd given them to me for a different spell, one I had no intention of casting. A spell that also needed—

"Shit."

Ari looked to where I was pointing in the spellbook. *The blood of a white fox,* it said.

"This spell needs it, too." I pressed my lips together. There had to be another way.

"Wait." Ari pointed to the bottom of the page, where in smaller script a note read: *If the spell's hold is not too tight, strong drink may substitute for blood.*

"How the hell are we supposed to know if the spell's hold is too tight?"

Ari shrugged. "I don't know, but I think it's good you didn't spill all that mead."

I pulled the mead from the pack. It felt about half full. Would pouring it into a bowl count as spilling it? Freki's warning had been against letting it touch the earth. At least we knew it was strong.

It had to work. No way was I casting the spell otherwise.

Ari frowned. "What if we call your Jared, have him call my mom and ask her what to do?" Ari pulled his phone from his pocket and opened it. His frown deepened. "Battery's dead."

I returned the notebook and the mead to the pack. The fog remained thick around us. My eyelids grew heavy. I closed them, saw flames behind my lids, and forced them open again. I didn't want to dream.

Ari glanced at my hands. They were shaking. "We'll figure it out, Haley," he said.

There was no way he could know that, but even so, his words made me feel a little better. I rummaged through the pack and pulled out a chunk of bread. I broke it in half, handed one half to Ari, and bit fiercely into the other. Food made me feel better, too. We were both starved, even though we'd eaten only a few hours before. We quickly went through everything but the granola.

After what seemed like hours the fog finally began to

thin. The sun grew low. The fog turned from gray to an eerie yellow that coated the stones around us. The sun touched the horizon.

Without warning Ari started cursing. His hands fumbled at the zipper of his jacket. "It's the setting sun that causes it!" Ari scrambled to his feet, jacket halfway unzipped. I stood, too, reaching for him, but Ari shoved me back. "Get *away.*" His hands were all wrong, too large and too flat.

Ari gasped and fell to all fours. He threw back his head and roared, even as black leather flowed and melted. Leather gave way to fur, hands and feet to white paws, face to small eyes and long snout.

I didn't run, though that roar echoed inside my chest. "Ari?" I kept my gaze on his green eyes.

The bear stared at me, trembling. I trembled, too. I'd watched enough nature documentaries to know the damage a bear's claws could do. Yet a real polar bear would have attacked me by now.

The bear whirled from me and ran, disappearing over the stones into the fog.

"Ari!" I fumbled in my pockets for his handkerchief and realized he'd taken it back. I grabbed my pack and ran after him, shouting the words Svan had spoken:

> *May you shed this form and show*
> *Your true self.*
> *I will fear no bear-kin!*

I stopped short and waited. Ari didn't return. Had he even heard? I made my way back to the roadside and sank to the ground. Maybe if I stayed in one place, Ari could find me. I drew my arms around my knees and rocked back and forth. *Alone.* Now I really was alone.

Darkness thickened around me. A bright moon rose, turning the fog silver. There wasn't any wind. In the silence, the world seemed eerie and strange.

It wasn't like anyone could hurt a bear, even if they could see him. Ari would be *fine*.

Damp fog tickled my neck. I suddenly wanted Mortimer, my stuffed wombat, more than anything. I thought of Mom, sewing and re-sewing all my stuffed animals for me. My chest felt tight.

My eyes began to close. I used my fingers to prop them open. No way did I want to dream here, alone in the dark and the fog. My heavy lids felt gritty and sore. I *had* to rest them, just for a moment.

It felt good to close my eyes, but that was okay—I just wouldn't sleep.

I stood on a hillside beside a tower of gray blocks riddled with cracks. The sky was thick with clouds, the air silent and still, not a bird in sight. Quiet. Peaceful. I'd stop the dream right here. I could stop it wherever I wanted.

A burning arrow flew through the air. I knew when that arrow landed, it would burn the world—No! I reached up and caught the arrow in my hand. It burned, but I wasn't afraid of pain.

For a heartbeat, two heartbeats, everything was okay. Then a spark caught, somewhere inside me, a spark of fire that rose to meet the fire I held. Fire roared through my blood and burst through my skin. Cracks opened beneath my feet as I screamed. The fissures stretched on and on, toward the edge of the sea.

"*Free,*" a rough voice whispered, and the words burned, too. "*We will be free!*"

I woke with a start, still screaming, drenched in sweat. The mist felt stiflingly hot. I leaped to my feet and backed away, knowing that even awake, I couldn't escape my dreams. I heard a snuffling sound behind me, and I whirled around.

A huge white bear stared at me, bright in the moonlit fog, shaking as hard as I was. I looked at him. He looked back through bright green eyes.

"Ari?" My throat hurt from screaming.

The bear bowed his head. He lumbered toward me, then stopped, uncertain. I reached out and touched his wet nose, even as I thought about how stupid it was to just walk up and touch a bear—to touch any wild animal.

But Ari still wasn't acting like a wild animal, and all my classes and internships and Web surfing had never covered bears who were also boys, anyway. *How could they leave out a thing like that?* I gave a strained laugh. It turned into a sob, and once I started sobbing I couldn't stop.

Ari nudged my chest with his muzzle. I threw my arms around his thick neck, still sobbing. His fur was cold and damp. I clung to it, feeling the burning memory of my dream subside. "How the *hell* did either of us get into this mess?" I demanded. Ari had no answer to that. "I was afraid you wouldn't come back," I said, and cried until I couldn't cry anymore.

I curled up on the ground then, and Ari stretched out beside me, watching me still. The fog was clearing at last, and up above the moon shone so brightly it hurt my eyes. I closed them and buried my face in Ari's cool white fur, which felt coarse and soft and slippery all at once. I started drifting off, too tired to stop myself, even though maybe Svan's spell to turn Ari human would have worked now.

"You're not Mortimer," I whispered to Ari, "but you'll do."

I slept once more, and for the first time since having arrived in Iceland—the first time since my mother had disappeared—I had no dreams.

⌒ *Chapter 13* ⌒

I woke to a cold blue sky. An arm was draped over me, not a bear's arm—a boy's. Ari lay on his side, propped up on one elbow and staring at me through his human eyes as though he feared I'd disappear if he moved.

"You came back," I said.

"Once I was sure I wouldn't hurt you." Wind tugged at his white hair. "Once I knew it was me in control, and not the bear."

My throat still hurt, but I felt like I'd slept—really slept—for the first time in ages. "Thank you," I whispered.

Ari's mouth quirked into a smile. "So I managed to do something right, then?"

I made a strangled sound, half a laugh and half a sob. I put my hands slowly to his face and pressed my lips to his.

181

Heat rose in me. I didn't know if it came from my magic or not. Ari's lips were so soft. I reached for his hair, remembering that it was soft, too, as soft and coarse as his polar bear fur.

Ari drew away with a gasp and sat up. His own hands shook as he looked at me. "No," he said, but he sounded uncertain.

What did he mean, *no*? I sat up, too. I remembered falling asleep, buried in his fur. He hadn't minded then. "You didn't mind in Muninn's mountain."

Ari looked right at me. "I didn't know you had a boyfriend then."

He was right, I knew he was right—I didn't want him to be right. What was wrong with me? Was I no better than Dad? "You chased the nightmares away." I looked down, realizing how stupid that sounded.

Ari shut his eyes, as if my words had hurt him. "I won't be the reason you break up with him."

"I wouldn't—"

"And if you don't break up with Jared, I won't be that guy you feel guilty about and try to pretend never happened. I'd rather go a little longer between girlfriends than be someone else's stupid mistake. Or maybe you'd tell yourself I don't count, because it was only Iceland, thousands of miles from your home—no, Haley." He sounded more sure now.

"I'd never pretend you didn't count," I said, but I

couldn't argue with the rest. I wanted to, though. Just like I wanted to kiss him again, not caring if it made sense or not. I jammed my hands into my pockets. The knuckles of my right hand brushed burning metal. The fire in me rose in response. I cursed and pulled my hands out, filling my mind with thoughts of cool moonlit polar bear fur. The heat subsided.

"Are you okay?" Ari asked.

"I'm *fine*," I snapped.

Ari looked away from me. He pulled his cell phone from his pocket and fiddled with it, as if the battery might decide it wasn't really dead. Had Jared tried to call, after the battery had died?

It had taken Jared and me years to fall in love. How could I fall for Ari after only a few days? I got to my feet and pulled my backpack over my shoulders.

Ari shoved the phone back into his pocket, not looking at me. "We should start walking."

I pictured hours and hours of walking, not looking at Ari, trying not to wonder what it would feel like to hold his hand, to touch his hair. I got to my feet and pulled on my backpack. "Let's *run*," I said, and burst into a jog without waiting for Ari to answer.

The pack bounced on my back—I didn't care. Muscles stiff with sleep loosened as I ran, and I settled into a comfortable lope beside the water. Dirt turned to pavement—real pavement—beneath my feet. Around me the gray stones were bright with autumn moss. Snow streaked the distant hills.

Behind me I heard Ari breathing hard. I slowed down, into the easier pace I used when running with Jared. *It doesn't matter,* I told myself as my feet slapped the pavement, not sure if I meant Jared or Ari or both of them. All that mattered was getting to Hlidarendi, returning the coin, and figuring out what to do about the fire in me—if anything *could* be done about that.

Ari caught up, his face red, sweat dripping from his hair. "This was easier"—he gasped—"as a bear."

I dropped to a brisk walk, knowing that if I went any slower my legs would cramp up. I pulled off my jacket. My skin felt warm and flushed, in spite of the cool breeze, but it was good heat, for once. Normal heat, like after any run.

Ari wiped a hand across his sweaty face. We reached another intersection, and he turned left, so that we were following the fjord out the other side. "I guess it's true— what they say. About American girls—being fast—"

I thwapped him with my jacket. Ari laughed. "Hey, I'm not the one who set that pace!" He took off his jacket, too, and draped it over his shoulders. "Maybe if I just keep it off I'll stay human. Do you think it could be that easy? I didn't even know the coat was bearskin until Muninn said so."

I wrapped my jacket around my waist. "What's it like?" I asked. "Being a bear?"

Ari looked down at the pale white hairs on the backs of

his hands. We passed a farmhouse. A pair of black-capped terns perched on the roof, watching us. "I could have killed him, you know. The sorcerer."

"No one would blame you for that." I kicked a black stone down the road. The volcanic rock was lighter than I'd expected. It disappeared into the distance.

"You don't understand. I would have enjoyed it. It would have been fun."

The memory of falling asleep in his soft fur made me want to cry. "You didn't hurt me."

"This time." Ari made a fist and slowly opened it, as if fascinated by the way his own fingers worked. "This isn't like some cartoon where the bears are all funny and cuddly with googly Disney eyes."

"Don't you think I know that?" We caught up with my rock. I picked it up and stared at its air-pocked surface. Ari watched me, his skeptical look making clear he thought I still didn't understand. "Listen, Ari, I know a few things about polar bears—real polar bears. They don't turn and run just because they're scared they might hurt someone. They don't wait to come back until they're sure they won't, either. They don't run at all, not unless they're chasing down prey."

Ari kicked a patch of moss at the side of the road. "It's still dangerous. If I get angry as a bear, it's worse than as a human."

"This whole mess we're in is dangerous." I glanced at Ari's hands. His palms were still very faintly red where I'd burned him. "If anyone should be worried about being dangerous, it's me."

Ari scowled. "That's not the same thing."

"No." I let the rock fall. "Because you can't bring buildings down with *your* magic. Maybe you were right to run away."

"Don't be stupid," Ari said.

"I won't if you won't." I drew a breath. "You know, if we can't fix the memory thing, I won't run home to America when this is all done. I won't leave you alone here."

Ari shrugged uncomfortably. "You don't have to stay because you feel sorry for me."

"Idiot!" I almost kicked him. "I wouldn't stay because I felt sorry for you." He didn't want to kiss me—he might even be right about that—but that didn't mean we weren't friends, or that being friends wasn't important. "I won't abandon you." *Not when you're a bear, and not when you're human, either.* "Jared would agree, you know."

"That you should stay here with me instead of him?" Ari laughed. "I doubt that."

"That friends don't abandon each other," I said sharply.

A truck rumbled along the road behind us. We moved onto the shoulder as it passed. Wind blew the grasses at our feet and rippled the surface of the fjord. Ari jammed his hands into his pockets as we walked on. "The thing is," he said slowly, "if it turns out I change every night, with or without the jacket? Even if we fix everyone's memories, I have a problem then. Hard to go to college as a bear—never mind getting a job or playing gigs."

Maybe you could stick to matinees. That wouldn't work in Iceland, though, where the winter days were as short as the summer nights. "You could migrate. Like an arctic tern." I stifled a giggle. "Sorry. I shouldn't joke."

"Of course you should joke." Ari shook his white hair out of his eyes. "Hey, I could be the first polar bear at the South Pole. Go visit the penguins. What do you think?"

"I think there are no penguins at the South Pole, only at the coast." I laughed, and Ari laughed, too. I pulled the granola from my pack, and we ate it as we continued on. We veered away from the water for a bit, then turned left, leaving the main road behind. A harbor town came into view below us. The bright red- and blue-roofed houses reminded me of my run through Reykjavik, what seemed a lifetime ago.

We came to a small gas station. Wind whistled through its broken windows, and the door swung open on its hinges. I rubbed my bare arms, though the wind still didn't seem cold to me. How far away had the earthquake been felt?

A girl and boy on bicycles circled around the parking lot while a woman stood nearby, talking into a cell phone. Across the road, I saw more emergency vehicles beside a huge orange tent. A few people sat in lawn chairs by the tent, talking quietly. Down toward the harbor, I saw smaller tents in some of the yards, as well as more people talking in the streets. It didn't *look* like anyone was hurt, but the hurt people wouldn't have been standing around outside, would they?

"This is my fault," I said.

Ari gave my hand a quick squeeze. "Not only yours. Come on, let's see if we can find a bus schedule." He started toward the gas station door.

The boy on the bicycle headed the same way, not seeing us. We quickly stepped out of his path, but then the bicycle hit a rock, and he tumbled to the ground.

Ari and I ran to his side, even as the girl stopped pedaling. I reached for the boy to help him up. He flinched as if burned, burst into tears, and ran wailing to the woman. She flipped her phone closed and stroked his hair.

The girl sat on her bicycle, balanced on her toes. She looked right at us. I smiled, even though she couldn't see us.

She smiled back. "Are you ghosts?" she asked solemnly.

I started. "I—I don't know." Was the spell broken? No, the boy hadn't seen me, though he'd felt my touch.

The girl nodded, still solemn. "I see ghosts. My grandma says some people can." She reached into her pocket and offered me a piece of black licorice.

I took it. "Thank you," I said.

"You're welcome!" She turned and pedaled away, winding through the parking lot toward the woman and boy.

I tore the licorice in half, gave a piece to Ari, and popped the other into my mouth. It was salty. My lips scrunched up, but then I decided I liked it. "A gift," I whispered. Unlike with Muninn or Svan or the fire spirits, there'd been no price—it was just a gift.

A pair of backpackers headed down the road and into the parking lot. They walked over to the woman. "Do you know—is there a bus today?" one of them asked in English.

The woman answered in English, more stilted than the Icelandic she'd spoken on the phone. "The bus is canceled. Because of the earthquake."

Ari and I looked at each other. The woman asked the backpackers where they were headed; Akureyri, they said, and she opened her phone, saying she knew someone who might be able to give them a ride.

We could hitch a ride, too, sneak into someone's backseat, only how would we know where they were going? Up above a gray falcon circled around, reminding me of the kids on their bicycles. Could we borrow bicycles and head south that way?

Ari took his jacket from his shoulders and stared at it thoughtfully. Wind pulled at the sleeves and at his hair. "Ah, well," he said at last. He pulled the jacket back on and zipped it up. "There's enough time to be human later."

I gave him a puzzled look. Ari held out a hand and bowed slightly.

"Haley," he said, "may I offer you a ride?"

～ *Chapter 14* ～

It took me a moment to realize what Ari meant. "As a bear?"

"I may not be much as a human, but as a bear I make pretty good time." He grinned. "Or if you prefer, we could hotwire a car. Not that I've ever done that before, but they do it in movies all the time, so how hard can it be?"

"No, no, I'd love a ride. That'd be amazing, actually." *How many wildlife biologists get to ride a polar bear?* Jared would be jealous—I cut the thought off. *If he's jealous, it won't be because of the bear.* "Are you sure?" I asked Ari. "I mean, it's awfully far."

"Of course. It'll be just like shooting womp rats back home." At my blank look, Ari said, "Another *Star Wars* joke. I'm a bit of a geek, if you hadn't noticed. Yes, I'm sure.

I have lots more energy as a bear. More than I know what to do with, actually. I can get us to Hlidarendi."

"Thanks," I said. *We really are in this together,* I thought.

We loaded up on sandwiches and Cokes and maps at the abandoned gas station. We tried to call Jared on the pay phone there, too, but like at the hotel, we didn't get a dial tone. Ari left a few bills on the counter to pay for all we took—though we still had no idea whether anyone could see our money—and then we headed down to the harbor to wait for the sun to set and Ari to change. We stretched out on a patch of grass. Ari studied the map. I took out Thorgerd's spellbook and studied the spell for returning the coin. There were words I had to speak—after my third pathetic attempt to sound them out, Ari took pity and read them for me. I repeated the words until I had them memorized.

Ari folded up the maps. "I know the way. I won't screw this up."

"You didn't screw anything up." I stopped reciting the spell under my breath and looked at him. "Seriously."

Ari looked back. For a moment we stared at each other, frozen in place. More than anything, I wanted to take his face in my hands, to convince him without words that he hadn't messed up after all. Did he have any idea how much harder this all would be without him?

"I didn't kiss you when I had the chance. If that isn't screwing up, I don't know what is." Ari turned abruptly toward the harbor. The water was bright beneath the afternoon sun.

I wanted to tell him—what? That he still had a chance? That he didn't, but I wished he did? I bit down hard on my inner lip, drawing blood. It tasted coppery and hotter than blood should have.

I pulled a sandwich from my pack and bit fiercely into it. The taste of blood mixed with the taste of tuna salad and a yellow sauce that was more like mayo than mustard. I read through the spell once more.

The mead has to work. "Ari, your mom was going to cast this spell. She wouldn't have killed a fox— would she?"

Still looking at the water, Ari pulled a Coke from my pack and popped it open. "You're asking me? I didn't think Mom would sleep with a married man." Ari picked up a flat rock and skipped it over the blue water. "You know, when I invited myself to lunch at Thingvellir, I had this idea that maybe you'd figured things out—about my mom and your dad, I mean—better than me. Stupid, really. I don't know why I thought they'd have even told you when they didn't want me to know, either."

I tried to skip a stone, too, but it sank right into the water. I watched the ripples circle out. Maybe I was the stupid one, for not having figured out what was going on sooner.

We finished the sandwiches as twilight settled in. Ari stood and handed me the flashlight. I stood as well.

He stretched and took a few steps back. "Ready?" A small smile crossed his face. *He's looking forward to this.*

As the sun dipped behind the hills, the smile faded. Ari's eyes took on a wide, startled look. "You'd think I'd get used to this—" His voice turned hoarse as his jacket began to flow, his face to twist and change, his skin to sprout white fur. Within moments a white bear stood roaring before me. The sound sent shivers down to my bones. Somewhere deep inside I *knew* I ought to run.

Ari whirled and ran from me instead, loping away alongside the harbor. I raced after him, calling his name. He disappeared into the distance as the sky grew dimmer. I stopped and took a deep breath. *He'll come back. Just like last night.* Did he need to remember that he wouldn't hurt me? Or to wait until it was true?

"Get back here," I whispered. I heard a distant roar.

A streak of white loped toward me through the dimness. Ari stopped just an arm's length away, sides heaving. He hunkered down and rested his head in his paws, looking sheepish.

I laughed. "You just had to get that out of your system, didn't you?"

Ari lifted his head and tilted it to one side. I could almost see his quirked smile in the gesture. I reached out and rubbed his nose.

He sneezed, covering my hand with polar bear snot. "Was that *really* necessary?" I asked.

Ari stood and gave me a long look down the length of his snout. I wiped my hand on his fur, and Ari nudged my hand away. "Hey! Not my fault you forgot to give me your handkerchief!"

Ari gave me another look—somehow, I knew he was laughing, too. He crouched down and waited for me to mount. I tightened the straps on my backpack and climbed up.

Or tried to. I immediately slid from his slick back to the ground. I cursed and got to my feet, brushing dirt and grass from my clothes. Ari turned his head to look at me.

"You think it's funny, don't you?"

The bear nodded, a human gesture. I swatted him on the nose. Ari snorted, blowing more snot onto my jacket. I rolled my eyes and tried to climb onto his back again. This time I didn't fall off until Ari began moving.

It took five tries in all. Finally I got myself up over his broad shoulder blades, leaning forward and grabbing handfuls of the loose skin around his neck to hang on.

He started slowly, first with a lumbering walk and then, when I didn't fall off this time, a slow lope. We made our way back through the streets of the town as I adjusted my balance. The water rippled gently behind us.

"Ghosts!" a voice shouted. I looked up. The girl from the gas station stood beside the road, holding her bicycle with one hand. She laughed and waved. I smiled, wondering why she could see us. Maybe it was like she'd said—some people just could. Just like some people could turn into bears, and others got caught by spells they didn't expect. Maybe the world was just a strange, strange place, and there was nothing anyone could do about it.

"Run, ghosts!" the girl called, laughing still. Ari broke into a faster, springier run.

Wind whipped past me, fast and fierce, blowing my short hair from my face. I held on for dear life—hands clutching fur, legs pressed down against those shoulder blades—but then I laughed, too. Ari's spine coiled and uncoiled as his paws hit the shoulder of the road, and he seemed to spring forward—to *fly* forward—rather than to run. "Wow," I said. "Just—wow."

Ari ran faster, leaving Holmavik behind as he returned to the main road. The wind got down beneath my jacket and up inside my sleeves. It cut through my jeans, but I didn't care. I didn't even care that it was the fire inside me that kept me warm. Running had never been anything like this. When I ran, I always knew I wasn't really flying, that my feet could only leave the ground for too-short instants.

We flew past barren rocks and windblown autumn grasses. The road wound around to follow a broad bay. Pavement gave way to dirt, dirt to more pavement. The moon rose and the stars came out, impossibly bright. The horizon began to shiver and glow.

I stiffened, remembering dreams of fire rising from the earth, but this fire wasn't orange. A curtain of shimmering light rose from the edge of the sky, unearthly ripples of red and green. "An aurora," I whispered. The northern lights, so beautiful—the laughter caught in my throat. *Dad would love this. Mom, too.*

Ari stopped and looked up. In the sudden stillness we watched the curtain blow across the sky, as if in some un-felt wind. Too beautiful—tears streamed down my face. I suddenly missed Mom more than anything. I buried my face in Ari's fur, which smelled faintly of the sea. When I looked up again, the light was fading, the world turning silver with moonlight.

Ari took off again, sticking to the shoulder of the road when he could, running on pavement when he had to. The road veered inland along a deep fjord, wound back out to sea, then followed a second fjord. The hills turned lower and gentler. A horse with a shaggy mane and big brown eyes whirled and ran from us, whinnying a warning. Like the girl in Holmavik, apparently the horse could see ghosts.

We entered a deeper, broader fjord, this one filled with thin fog. At an intersection Ari slowed a moment, then chose an unpaved road over a paved one, following a river valley away from the water. The fog stayed with us, not as thick as last night's fog, and the land grew flatter. Ari began breathing harder, slowing down a little. I leaned toward one of his small ears. "Do you need a rest?" I asked.

He nodded his shaggy head and slowed to a stop. I slid from his back. My hips were sore from stretching across his shoulders, and my hands ached from holding on. I walked to keep from cramping up, stretching my fingers one by one and rubbing my palms. Ari lumbered close beside me, a comforting presence.

I turned on the flashlight. Mist made the blue light eerie and strange. Farmhouses dotted the land, their windows dark. Signs by the road named the farms as we passed them: Hornsstadir, Hoskuldsstadir. At a bend in the road, just past the sign for Hrutsstadir, an old man stood alone, gazing into the dark. His hair was white, his gaze sharp. He wore a belted shirt and leather-wrapped pants, just like Svan. I stared at him, and like the girl he looked right back at me.

"I know your eyes," he said.

"What?" Mist curled between us. "You can see me."

"You and your tame berserk, yes." The man chuckled, but then his face grew grim. "I see many things, and little good comes from most of them. I saw you when my niece was born, though I did not know it at the time, and so I said she had the eyes of a thief. But your eyes tell me that you see things, too. Seeing the future runs in our family."

Ari tilted his head, as if he'd figured something out, but the words meant nothing to me. Not until the man added, "You are heading to her home. In the south."

I backed away then. The last thing I wanted was to get tangled up with another one of Hallgerd's uncles.

"Truly, Haley, I mean you no harm."

I stopped short. How did he know my name? He

stepped forward and reached for me, but his hand went right through mine, just like Hallgerd's once had. *Ghost.* Which of us was the ghost here?

The man shrugged, as if used to this. "Time is an uncanny thing, as you know well enough. Have a care in the south. Whatever you steal, be sure to give it back again."

Did he mean Hallgerd's coin? I hadn't stolen that, but I hoped to give it back, anyway. How much did this man know about the coin? "What do you know about fire magic?" Maybe *he* could help get rid of the fire in me.

"I know less than you do, I think." There was sympathy in the man's eyes, and also a strange sort of sorrow. "The gift you've received will not be cast cheaply aside, but there is no helping that. Good fortune go with you, and with Hallgerd, too. I never meant her harm, either." He turned away then and walked toward the faint outline of a nearby farmhouse. One step, then another, and he disappeared into the mist.

Ari nudged my hand with his warm nose. He looked like he wanted to say something, but then he shrugged his huge shoulders and knelt down for me to mount. As I did I thought, *At least it can be cast aside. That's something, right?*

The road wound left and south, away from the river and out of the valley. The fog gave way to a cloudy sky that barely let the moonlight through. A few cars passed, and their engines seemed unnaturally loud.

In the distance, a plume of steam rose from the ground,

like the steam I'd seen when Dad and I drove to Thingvellir. The coals in me flared suddenly hot. I forced the flames
down—*tried* to force them down. This time, they didn't listen, and the fire in me burned cheerfully on. Fear rippled
through me.

We passed more plumes of steam. Heat spread through
my chest, my arms, my legs. I couldn't douse this fire.
I fought not to panic instead. The scent of sulfur tinged the
wind. I felt the heat beneath the road, the molten under-
ground rivers that fed the steam. I buried my face in Ari's
fur. The fire in me cooled, but only a little.

We flew past sweeping black hills and alongside rivers.
I wondered how Ari could keep running for so long. My
arms and hips ached. I shut my eyes a second to rest them.

*Fire roared before me. A flaming arrow—the earth
cracked open where it landed. The crack spread, like a tear
in a sweater. Molten fire bubbled through it, overflowing
into the land around it.*

I felt my grip slipping and jerked awake with a gasp.
Ari slowed and turned to look at me. "I'm okay," I told
him. "Just keep going." *Don't stop now.*

Ari ran on, and I clutched his fur tighter than I needed
to. My hands were slick with sweat. The wind burned
against my skin. In a distant corner of my mind I saw more
arrows, all aflame, landing throughout Iceland—south,
west, east, north. I saw arrows flying beyond the island, too,
landing in places I knew from maps: Greenland. England

and Norway. The northeastern United States. Wherever the arrows landed, cracks spread, tearing the land apart.

Seeing the future runs in our family. "That'd better not be the future." I imagined the cracks in the earth spreading all the way to Tucson—all the way around the world. I'd always assumed that whatever happened here, home would be safe.

Would returning Hallgerd's coin stop those arrows— stop that future? Or would it only give her more power, like Svan said? What if I needed to get rid of the fire in me to make the arrows stop?

We topped a rise. I looked down, over a glimmering lake and row after row of blocky stone walls. *I dreamed of a tower made of a child's gray blocks.* "Thingvellir," I said. This was where it all began.

Where it all ended, for Mom. I clutched Ari's fur so hard my knuckles turned white.

I felt once more the fire flowing beneath the earth. I felt the fire burning through my veins. Somehow, I kept that fire beneath my skin. Ari ran faster. Sweat poured down my face. A few figures—ghosts like Hallgerd's uncle—glanced up as we ran by. We left the lake and the ghosts behind, making our way past fields of gravelly black rock and through farmland broken up by farmhouses and small towns.

Ari stumbled, caught himself, and stumbled again. I stroked his fur. "Just a little further," I said, hoping it was true.

Ari put on a final burst of speed as we left another town

behind and headed into a broad valley. Grassy hills rose to our left, and a rocky field stretched out to our right. Ari wove around a herd of sheep that were sleepily crossing the road. Unlike the horse, the sheep didn't seem to see us.

The horizon turned gray. Drizzle fell, sizzling as it hit my hot skin. *Not panicking, not panicking . . .* The rain rolled right off Ari's white fur. He slowed down to look at a road sign. I shined the flashlight on it. Ari nodded and sped back up. Several more times he slowed to read signs and squint at the farmhouses beyond them.

Abruptly the pavement ended. The sky was brighter now, and I didn't need a flashlight to see the sign at the roadside: Hlidarendi, it read. Ari turned left and headed up a steep gravel lane, damp with rain. Around us, yellow and orange grasses were dotted with dandelions gone to seed. Raindrops clung to their fuzzy white tops. We passed another farmhouse, rounded a bend, and headed toward a small red-roofed church. On the slopes beyond it I saw more farmhouses.

Bright light broke through the dripping gray clouds. Ari staggered, and his fur rippled beneath my hands. I lost my grip and slid to the ground, even as Ari shrank, fur withdrawing into skin, head and arms and legs all pulling back, reshaping themselves into a human face, human limbs. In moments Ari's white hair was all that remained of the bear he'd been. He crouched on all fours, looking at me. I couldn't tell whether his skin was drenched with sweat or rain.

"Sorry," he said. "I guess you'll have to walk—the last few meters—" He tried to stand, but crumpled to the ground.

"Ari!" I knelt beside him, ignoring the fire that burned on in me, ignoring sore hips and aching hands and the rain that continued to fall. His eyes were closed. I leaned close to his lips to make sure he was breathing.

Ari's eyes fluttered open, and he gave a shaky smile. "Don't tempt me, yeah?" He slowly sat up. "I'm okay. Just— a little tired." His breath came out in gasps.

I remembered Svan talking about berserks. *Strong enough during a change, not much use after.* "Can you stand?"

"I can," Ari said. "But I—would rather—not if—it's all—the same to you. Gunnar's home is somewhere—past the church, I think. You should be able to make it—the rest of the way—on your own."

"Hell no. We got this far together. I'm not ditching you now."

"Being ditched doesn't sound—so bad. Just give me a few minutes."

I rubbed my arms. Through the nylon and fleece, I felt the heat from my skin. How long could I wait?

Something must have showed in my face, because Ari nodded grimly and draped his arm over my shoulders. His legs wobbled as I pulled him to his feet. He shivered in the thin light. "Your skin is burning, Haley."

"I know." I unzipped my jacket. The fire burned on, sweat plastering my T-shirt to my skin. Ari looked at me, but there wasn't anything I could *do* about it. I continued up the hill, dragging him with me. The path was steeper than it looked. My thighs ached as we climbed. Ari's legs trembled.

"What you did," I said as the rain kept falling around us, evaporating when it hit my skin. "That was amazing."

Tired as he was, Ari grinned. "It was, wasn't it? I think I could get used to being a bear." He stumbled; I caught him. "Only the hangover the next morning? That part sucks."

The gravel ended at a parking lot behind the church. From the roof, I heard chittering. A half dozen black-capped arctic terns were lined up there, staring at us through tiny eyes.

We walked faster, across the parking lot and up the hillside. Ari panted as we climbed through grasses slick with rain. Sheep grazed on the slopes above us. A stream trickled downhill a few dozen feet to our right, and a small wooden bridge arced over it. "I'm supposed—to go—here on—a class trip—next year. I don't know—the exact spot—where Gunnar and Hallgerd had their house. But there's a tourist sign." Ari gestured up the hill. "Maybe it's—close enough?"

The gray sky was bright, sun turning the clouds gold around the edges. I took a few steps toward the stream, stopped short, and looked around. "Here," I said.

"How can you know—"

"I *know* this hillside. I stood here in my dreams." Heat

rose in me as I remembered—blocks falling, fiery arrows striking the ground—this ground. I released Ari's arm to take off my backpack. He staggered and fell to his knees.

I knelt by his side. "You sure you're all right?"

Ari gave me a long look. "As sure as you are."

"Right." I tore off my jacket. Wind blew through my sodden T-shirt, but it felt hot as the desert wind back home. I drew the spellbook from my pack and laid out the ingredients for the spell: The mead. The bowl. The claw. The rock, which was softer than it looked, flaking at the edges. I left the knife in the pack—I didn't plan to use it. At last I reached for the coin. Its heat felt good against my burning skin, like a warm caress. I pulled it out.

As I did, the air filled with the beating of wings. I stood and whirled around, shoving the coin back into my pocket. Ari got to his feet by my side, though his legs still shook.

Muninn circled once around us, then landed on a rock beside my backpack. The terns fell silent. The clouds thickened, and the drizzle turned to a fine misting rain.

Not again, not now, I can't forget now—I didn't look into Muninn's eyes. *I'm Haley Martinez,* I thought fiercely. *Daughter of Gabe and Amanda*—

"Haley." Muninn's wingbeats were soft and slow. "I come to offer you a bargain."

~~ Chapter 15 ~~

"What bargain?" *I could run.* But Ari couldn't, and besides, even an ordinary raven flew faster than my fastest sprint.

The wind died. Scraps of mist hovered over the wet hillside. "A bargain to protect this land from the fire you hold."

"You can do that?" I looked into Muninn's eyes after all. Dizziness washed over me. "You can take the fire away?" Mist brushed my neck, but the cold was a surface thing. It couldn't sink into my skin or reach the fire that flowed beneath it.

"I cannot." The fine rain didn't seem to touch Muninn's feathers. "The bargains you made in the fire realm are your own. I cannot undo them. What I can do is take you out of this place. In my mountain, you'll be beyond the reach of those who would enter this world through your fire. The land will be safer if you are not in it."

"No." Ari grabbed my hand. His fingers felt cool around mine.

Muninn krawked—it sounded like a laugh. His bright gaze shifted to Ari. "And how do you like being a bear, boy?"

"I like it fine." Ari leaned on me to steady himself. "What about Haley? How safe will she be if she accepts your bargain?"

"Safer than she would be anywhere else." Mist drifted around the raven. "There are no spirits in my mountain to feed her fire, and in my halls she might find the knowledge to keep that fire from consuming her."

Like Mom had been consumed—but Hallgerd's magic had done that. I thought of those fiery arrows tearing gashes in the earth. "Would I have to forget again if I went with you?"

Muninn's wings stopped for a beat—a moment's hesitation. "No. And I'd return the memory of you to the wide land—a gift for a gift."

"So you're saying our parents can remember us just in time for us to disappear forever?" Ari swayed and tightened his grip on my hand. "Some gift."

"Don't be stupid," I said. "*You* wouldn't have to go."

Ari laughed softly. "Ah, but being stupid is what I'm good at. Always best to stick with our strengths. Of course

I'd go with you. I may not be much use in the rescue department, but I can get this much right. I won't abandon you, either."

I thought of how in my dreams I was the arrow, the fire that tore the earth open. "If I accept your offer, could I return the coin to Hallgerd first?"

Muninn's krawk was angry this time. "That other one is not as great a danger to this land as you are now. Even so, I'll not have you returning any part of her power to her. There is danger there, too. The coin is a part of our bargain. It comes with you. Do you accept?"

Even now, I trusted Hallgerd with magic less than I trusted myself. Hallgerd's magic already *had* killed. Yet she hadn't even seemed to want the coin when last we'd spoken. "Do I have a choice?" I asked Muninn.

"There's always a choice." The raven's wingbeats were slow, rhythmic. "Yet bear this in mind, Haley—if you refuse this bargain, I will do all I can to claim your memories once more."

"Which, as it turns out, is not very much," a voice said. I looked around and saw a small white fox crossing the bridge over the mist-shrouded river.

"Freki!" I said.

Freki calmly trotted over to stand at my feet. "You know you have no control over Haley's memories now, Muninn, any more than you had control over Hallgerd's memories once she made her bargain. The spirits that burned away Haley's hair burned away the veil over her memories as well. Those powers are older than you or I, and as you say—we have no sway over them."

Muninn's feathers puffed out. "This is none of your concern, Freki."

"Ah, but it is." The rain didn't touch Freki's fur, either. "Haley gave me a gift, and I may have the chance to repay her, this day. So I will wait. Make your decisions, Haley. Cast your spell, or choose not to cast it. Neither Muninn nor I may interfere."

I looked at Ari. He looked at me. I knelt down and hugged the little fox tightly. "I missed you," I whispered, and realized it was true.

Freki squirmed out of my arms. "I have done my job well, then."

"Do you think I should accept Muninn's bargain?"

"I cannot say," Freki told me. "Mostly because I do not know."

"The fate of the land is at stake," Muninn said with several short, sharp wingbeats.

"This is not the first time the fate of what matters most has rested on human choices." Freki curled up at my feet, resting his head on his paws. "None but our master sees the future in full, and the price he paid is not one that others can bear. Haley will do as she thinks best, and no one here knows what will happen after that."

Rain still fell, soaking through my jeans and steaming

back into the air. *No one knows what will happen.* If only we did know—then Mom never would have gotten on a plane to Iceland. Ari never would have told Mom—or me— the things that he did. I wouldn't have run from the things I was told. And Dad wouldn't have—I pushed that thought aside. "None of us know. We just do the best we can and hope we don't screw it up too badly."

"Yeah," Ari said with a wry smile. "That."

Whatever you steal, be sure to give it back again. Hrut's words—I had no idea whether he'd meant the coin when he spoke them. But Katrin had thought the coin should be returned to Hallgerd, too. Did I trust Katrin? I thought of her and Dad—then I thought of how Katrin had stayed up through the night for me, translating Icelandic words to English ones, doing everything she could so that I wouldn't face magic unarmed.

I thought of Thorgerd, Hallgerd's daughter, whose warnings and instructions Katrin had passed on. Thorgerd's descendants had remembered, for generation after generation, that the coin needed to be returned. There had to be some reason for that.

I hadn't destroyed the land or the world *yet.* Neither had Hallgerd. Maybe there was a reason for that, too.

I fished the coin out of my pocket and set it down beside the black fire stone. "Let's finish this," I said.

Ari nodded and handed me the spellbook. I read Thorgerd's instructions one more time, thinking of how it took a thousand years' worth of my ancestors—of Hallgerd's daughters—to get this book to me.

Muninn's wings flapped steadily as he watched me. The mist thickened. "If this goes badly," the raven warned me, "you *will* pay."

Ari handed me the mead. We exchanged a glance as I uncorked the skin. *If things are going to go wrong, this is the place.* Freki's whiskers twitched. The little fox turned away from me and began nosing through my backpack. I poured the mead into the bowl, careful not to splash any to the ground. The amber liquid was tinged faintly with red. I waited, but the mead didn't steam, and the ground didn't shake. I caught a whiff of its sweet scent, and tiredness washed over me.

I blinked the heaviness from my eyes and took Svan's raven's claw to my thumb. Piercing my skin with it was easy. The pain felt good, the way holding the coin had felt good. I squeezed my finger, and blood welled to the surface, along with a tiny wisp of smoke. The wind felt suddenly hotter.

I tossed the claw down and used my blood to draw the symbol from the spellbook on the black stone: a circle with three intersecting lines, the ends of each crossed by smaller circles and lines—the same symbol that was on the coin. The stone grew warm. A few more flakes chipped off as I dropped it into the mead. I dropped the coin into the liquid, too, and then I chanted the words I'd memorized from the spellbook:

Powers beyond the earth, hear me!
Powers beneath the earth, aid me!
Find her, turn her,
Return to her this gift!

The fire in me rose with the words, like flames to wind. The mead hissed and steamed. I thrust my hand into it. Flames leaped from the bowl, burning my skin. The scent of hot metal filled the air. I closed my eyes and saw more flames, the flames of my nightmares.

The flames I'd leaped through. Huge figures strode toward me, made entirely of fire, their arms and legs and necks bent at unnatural angles. One of them reached in my direction. I drew away, hot shudders racing through me. He wasn't reaching for me, though. He was reaching for the bowl in which the mead yet steamed. He dipped a fiery hand into the liquid, then jerked back with a roar.

"How dare you offer us the drink of our enemies? We refuse your gift!"

The flames in my blood burst through my skin. Pain— I'd never felt pain like this. My skin was melting, my bones were melting—I started screaming and couldn't stop. The ground buckled beneath me like a horse trying to throw me from its back.

Someone grabbed me. There was a roaring in my ears, and then—silence, save for the steady beating of wings.

I opened my eyes. Ari looked at me, his green eyes

wide, his hands shaking as he clasped my arms. The fire still burned in me, but it was contained—barely—beneath my skin once more. Liquid dripped from the hand I'd thrust into the mead, and the drips fell back into the bowl.

I drew my arms free, shook the last of the mead from my hand, and looked into the liquid. Somehow, impossibly, the earthquake—if there'd been an earthquake—hadn't spilled any. Maybe you couldn't spill mead like this by accident, or maybe the fire giants hadn't wanted to call on Freki and Muninn's master, either. "The mead was no good." My throat felt scratchy from screaming. "It just made them angry. The spell—"

"The spell isn't worth your life," Ari said.

What is this small life against the fate of the world? But if I'd died, the fire would have burst through my skin, out into that world.

Muninn's wings beat on. "Stupid girl! The power will never be contained now."

"I wouldn't be so sure of that." There was movement in my backpack. Freki backed out of it, holding the hilt of Svan's knife between his teeth.

We all turned to look at the fox. He dropped the knife in front of me. "Even had you offered more suitable brew, the fire's hold on you is too tight. A working as great as this one requires blood. I can give you that."

Muninn's wingbeats fell silent. I stared at Freki, not understanding—not wanting to understand.

"Haley," Freki said, "not long ago, you gave me a gift. Two gifts: a drink of sacred mead and the life of one of my kin. I would repay those gifts now."

A single sharp beat of Muninn's wings. "No."

"No!" For once I agreed with Muninn completely.

Freki tilted his head and said nothing.

"There's nothing to repay!" Wildness rose in me. Fire roared in my ears as I yelled, "It was a *gift*! You don't pay back a gift! That's not how it works!"

"The spell will consume you if you do not complete it." Freki nudged the sheathed blade with his nose.

"So let it consume me," I said.

"Hell no," Ari said.

"After the spell consumes you," Freki went on matter-of-factly, "its power will be set free into the world."

I shook my head. "I won't kill you. No way will I—" I looked wildly around. "If the spell needs blood, it can have mine!" I grabbed the knife out of its sheath and drew it toward my wrist. I had a lot more blood than Freki did. I might not even have to die.

"Oh, no, you don't." Ari tried to grab the knife. I wrenched it away from him and pressed the blade to my skin. It was sharp, and I was used to breaking skin. A thin line of blood welled up.

I smelled a burning sulfur smell. Paper-thin flames rose up out of the cut—out of my blood. I froze, clutching the knife, mesmerized by the sight. The ground trembled. I barely noticed. Such a pretty light—

Ari's hand clamped down over my wrist. The fire went out. The ground went still. I jerked my arm away from him. "How dare you—"

A sickening burned-skin smell stopped me mid-sentence. I looked down and saw puckered red skin around the cut. Pain seeped into my awareness slowly, like blood through a bandage. I felt the cut bleeding again, and I knew any moment fire would follow once more—my own blood burning, melting my skin. I doubled over and threw up in the grass, even as the pain in my wrist flared hotter. Burning hurt way, way more than breaking skin or drawing blood.

Ari grabbed my wrist and wrapped something around it. His handkerchief. I swallowed and sat up as the pain receded a little.

"So you see," Freki said calmly, "your blood will not do. It will only set the power free."

I smelled the handkerchief beginning to burn. Ari grabbed the water bottle out of my pack and poured it over the cloth. The burning smell subsided, replaced by the wet ash scent of an old campfire. Ari handed me the bottle, and I drank deeply, cool water soothing my throat. "I won't kill you," I told Freki again.

"Don't be silly, Haley." Freki laid a paw on my leg. "I cannot die. I will only leave this world for a time, nothing more. Even so, I do not offer this lightly."

My chest ached. "Will it hurt?"

Freki didn't answer, which was answer enough. Muninn's wings flapped sharply downward. "I will not allow it," the raven said.

The little fox laughed. "You have no power over me, Muninn. We've always been equals, in our master's eyes and all others'. This gift is mine to give."

To my amazement, Muninn didn't argue with that. He glowered at us all in complete silence.

I looked at Ari. Ari swallowed hard. He tore a blank page from his mother's spellbook and made it into a funnel, then sat down, balanced the mead skin between his knees, and used the funnel to pour the mead back into the skin. Nothing soaked through the waterproof paper. Not one drop hit the ground. In a few seconds the bowl was empty.

"You didn't want me to do this before," I said.

"Not so much depended on it then," Ari said grimly. He took the fire stone out of the funnel and set it on the ground. The black stone had my blood upon it still; the mead hadn't even smudged it. Ari set the coin on the ground, too, bouncing the silver in his palm as if it were hot. His skin was burned where he'd grabbed my wrist, a new welt across his palm and fingers already blistering.

"I hurt you."

"I'll survive," Ari said brusquely. "I'd like to see to it that you survive, too."

I looked down at Freki. He looked up at me. His tiny eyes were filled with compassion. "It is different for humans, I know," the fox said. "If you leave this world, you leave it forever, and there are those who would miss you if you did." He flicked an ear toward Ari, even as Ari muttered, "Damn right."

"Accept this gift, Haley. Erase the debt between us."

"There's no debt between us." My throat tightened around the words. I glanced at Ari. His lips were pressed together, his expression grim. If the fire beneath my skin destroyed me, he really would be alone here.

I thought of Dad, staying in Iceland, waiting for me. I thought of Jared in Tucson, waiting as well. What would they think if I never came back? Would Dad remember me at all?

Mom wouldn't want this. But I wasn't so sure. The thing about the animals at the clinic, Mom always said, was that they were helpless. They depended on us for everything. And wild animals were wild—they didn't understand. Freki was neither wild nor a pet.

It was because of Mom that I knew what it was like to have someone disappear and never return.

I wiped the sweat from my neck. My skin was fever-hot. "You swear you'll come back?" I asked Freki. "Eventually?"

"You have my word." The little fox glanced toward Muninn. "So long as you remember me in this world, I will return to it."

My throat hurt. "Of course I'll remember you."

Ari gave my hand a quick squeeze. I swallowed hard and reached for the knife.

Muninn gave an angry krawk and launched himself from the ground, flying up to the church. He perched beside the little birds. "Have a care, Haley."

I can't do this. I stroked Freki's head with my free hand. So soft—softer than bear fur, softer than anything I knew. He sat back and gazed at me through brown fox eyes, waiting. I moved my hand to his back and gently took hold of the scruff of his neck. Around my wrist, the handkerchief began to smolder. I brought the blade toward Freki's throat. My hand shook.

"Quickly, Haley, please."

I drew the knife across his fur, gasping as it bit the skin beneath. Yet that was only his skin—I pushed harder and felt a sickening pop as the blade severed the vessels beneath. Freki twitched, once, and was still. Muninn let out a piercing cry. And then hot blood spurted from the wound, onto my hand and sleeve. Its coppery scent was everywhere.

Ari shoved the bowl under the little fox to catch the blood, even as Freki's open eyes went dull. I dropped the knife and grabbed Freki's legs to hold him over the bowl. So much blood—it stopped spurting and began to pour from the wound, filling the bowl. Too soon it was done. The flow of blood slowed, then stopped. Freki hung limp in my hold, his white chest drenched with red. Hot tears burned down my face. What kind of monster was I?

"Don't you *dare* waste this gift!" Muninn's wings beat furiously at the air. Wind picked up around us, and the rain began falling again—had it ever stopped? I scratched Freki behind the ears one more time. "I'm sorry," I whispered, and laid him gently on the grass.

Ari's eyes were damp, too, but he just pointed to the stone and the coin. I dropped them both into the bowl and repeated the spell. This time the liquid began to boil.

I shoved my hand into it. The blood didn't seem so hot now—or maybe my skin burned just as hot. I shut my eyes and saw flames once more. A fiery hand reached into the liquid. I heard a deep, satisfied sound.

"*Ah. Better,*" the rough fire-voice said. "*Much better. We accept your gift. Cast your spell. We'll be ready for you and for your world, should you fail.*" A hot shudder ran through me at the words.

The flames rose higher. Through them I saw a clear sky with a broad path beneath it. I saw *back,* past the years of my own life, to a time before cars and airplanes, when homes were made of wood and grass, when dragon ships sailed the seas and cloth was woven on weighted looms. I saw stories released from their pages, not bound in books but free to be spoken and remembered. I saw—

My mother standing on the path, almost close enough to touch, her face streaked with angry tears. She looked up at me, and for a moment our eyes met. "Mom," I said, stunned, the heat that burned in me forgotten. Was it really her? The path pulled me toward her, and I reached out my hands.

My hands and gaze were wrenched away. "Mom!" I fought to look back, but the path pulled me on, past other women: the grandmother I barely knew, because she lived in Canada; the great-grandmother I'd met only in old photos; her mother and grandmother and great-grandmother in turn. The heat came with me. I feared if I looked at my hands I'd see not skin, but flame.

I saw beyond the oldest, crumbliest pictures to other women with fair hair and fair eyes. Each of them looked at me in turn, and then my gaze was pulled farther back, and farther still, for countless generations until—

"Haley!"

A kneeling woman glared up at me, holding a feathered arrow in one hand. She was older now, with lines around her eyes and mouth, but I knew her. I'd never forget her or what she'd done. She handed her arrow to someone out of sight, glaring still. Behind her the sky was hot blue, no sign of rain.

"Why do you seek me, Haley? I have left you to your life. Leave me to mine."

She never should have cast her spell if she wanted to be left alone. I drew the coin out of the blood, just like my spell said to do. "I've brought you a gift!" I called.

Hallgerd grabbed another arrow and pressed her lips together. *"Haley, don't you dare. Leave Gunnar and me to our fate. I have released my claim on the coin and spell. Your life and mine are linked no longer."*

"The hell they aren't." I thought of Mom, leaving for Iceland, saying she'd see me in a few weeks. I thought of Freki's limp body in my arms. I threw the coin to Hallgerd, as hard and as fast as I could. Only once she caught it would I be free of her and her magic.

Hallgerd didn't turn away. She couldn't turn away. *"You will* pay *for this,"* she whispered. Her hand fell open. The arrow clattered to the wooden floor beside her, and the coin landed in her palm. Her fingers closed around it.

A wave of dizziness washed over me. The path, the earth, the sky all trembled and gave way. I fell, and flames rose up all around me. My cry was lost beneath their roar.

Then all at once the world went still. I was kneeling on wooden boards, and the sun shone brightly above me. Fire burned in me yet—did I think I was burning before? That was nothing compared to the heat I felt now. There was a roaring in my ears, and the air around me shimmered. I looked down at my hands. They were old hands, worn with age. I wore a dress, not jeans, beneath a scarlet cloak. A pouch and small knife hung from my belt. My head felt strangely heavy. Long hair fell over my shoulders from beneath my—hat? Headdress? I reached up and touched a blond lock. It felt hot, even to me—I jerked my hand away.

My skin was hot, too, fire burning through the blood beneath it.

Through the roaring, I heard yelling down below. I was in a small loft, above a long narrow house. One side of the peaked roof had been torn away, leaving open air ahead of me. Beside me, a ladder led down to another room.

A man knelt by the loft's open edge, sweat beading on his brow, a nocked bow in his hands. Beneath his leather shirt his arms were thick with muscle. Damp red hair, just beginning to gray, escaped from beneath his metal helmet. A grassy hillside rose ahead of us, like the hillside Ari and I had climbed, only now it was outlined by a bright blue sky, no sign of rain. Sheep grazed there, and the air held an earthy barnyard smell.

In my head Hallgerd cried, *"How dare you deny me my right to die by his side!"*

I started cursing then. Because the spell wasn't just for returning the coin. Katrin's spellbook had it wrong, or else after a thousand years a few things had been forgotten. I'd cast—must have cast—the same spell Hallgerd tried to cast at Mom, or one very much like it.

I was in Hallgerd's place, a thousand years ago. The man beside me was her husband, Gunnar, and he was—we were—under attack.

~ *Chapter 16* ~

The dizziness I felt now had nothing to do with the fire in me. It was panic—pure, burning panic. Gunnar fired his bow. An arrow whooshed through the air, and someone cried out down below. He reached back toward me for another arrow. I forced my panic down and handed it to him. Fire roared in me. Not only my fire. Somehow I knew I held Hallgerd's fire as well. Too much heat. Any second it would burst through my skin—and my hair. My hands shook, one of them clutching the burning coin I'd thrown.

Gunnar saw their trembling. "My brave Hallgerd," he said, though I was sure I seemed anything but brave. His eyes turned pleading, yet tender, too. I'd seen Dad look at Mom that way, when I was younger. "Go away from this place. No one will stop you from leaving. Be safe, my love."

I shook my head—because I wasn't his love, because I was a thousand years from anything safe—and handed him another arrow, trying not to look at the long drop down where the missing half of the roof should have been.

The air wavered with heat. I cried out at a sudden movement, even as Gunnar shot at the hand that reached over the edge. The hand lost its grip, and the man hit the ground below with a thud. I handed Gunnar another arrow, and another. The roaring in my ears went on. The air grew heavy with the smell of sweat and dirt. There was a long cut along one of Gunnar's sleeves, and the fabric around it was dark with clotted blood.

"*Give me the coin,*" Hallgerd hissed in my head. "*Let me return to him.*" For just a moment, my sight blurred and I saw the path between Hallgerd and me.

She was supposed to hate Gunnar. The story said so. She wasn't supposed to want to stay by his side.

Sweat made my burning hair cling to my neck. I kept handing Gunnar arrows, clutching the coin tightly in my other hand. I'd returned it, just like the spellbook said. Only the spellbook hadn't told me what to do after that. If I threw the coin to Hallgerd again would we be back where we'd started, with me holding the coin in my own time?

Another hand reached over the roof, but Gunnar shot it as well. Sweat poured down his face and stained his heavy leather tunic.

"*Haley,*" Hallgerd said. Her voice was suddenly, eerily

calm. *"It is a funny thing about berserks. They are so strong in their animal forms, but so weak afterward. And I see you have left me your knife."*

"Ari." I'd left him with Hallgerd. The fear in me turned up another notch, and the heat in me rose with it.

"Return to me my life, Haley, and I'll return yours to you." Once more I saw the path between Hallgerd and me, generations of ancestors between us.

I wasn't even supposed to be here. I was only supposed to return the coin. Maybe I hadn't really done that yet. Maybe I *needed* to throw it to Hallgerd again. I drew my hand back, knowing the spell was still alive between us.

A sharp twang brought me back to where I was. Gunnar dropped his bow—its string had snapped—and grabbed a long-handled axe, swinging it at the man who was climbing into the loft, sword in hand. Gunnar's blade connected with the man's neck. Blood spurted everywhere—on Gunnar's face and clothes, on the wooden planks, on my cloak. The man fell backward off the edge, hands grasping the air even as he died.

I braced my hands against the floor. Fire roared in me, around me. The stench of sweat and blood was everywhere. Through the roaring, I heard Gunnar's voice. "Hallgerd," he called. "Give me two locks of your hair. Twist them into a bowstring for me." There was a hint of strain in his voice now. Another man came over the wall. Gunnar swung at him, and the man fell away.

My hair—this was where Gunnar was supposed to die. This was where Hallgerd killed him.

Hell no. I wasn't Hallgerd. I didn't have to follow her script. If Gunnar wanted a few locks of hair, he could have them. I shoved the coin into the pouch at my belt and reached for the small knife. *Hang in there a little longer, Ari.*

"Yes, Haley," Hallgerd said. "*Whatever Gunnar needs, give it to him. Don't you dare let him die.*"

What? Hallgerd wasn't supposed to *agree* with me. I grabbed a lock of long blond hair and drew the knife close.

The hair *burned*—hot as liquid glass, hot as spun fire. Sparks flew from the strands. I let them go. "*Free,*" a rough voice whispered in my head. "*We will be free.*"

"*Do not lose courage now,*" Hallgerd's more human voice said. "*It will not burn your hands long, that hair into which the giants bound their power long ago. Only so long as it takes to string Gunnar's bow.*"

"Oh God." A bow strung with fire. That fire lighting arrows and opening molten cracks in the earth as the arrows fell. The fire spirits had bound their magic into my blood, but, for Hallgerd, they'd bound it into her hair. They'd even said so. If I gave that fire to Gunnar's bow—I felt ill all over again.

I couldn't do it. Even without my dreams, I knew it down to my bones. The arrow fired from such a bowstring would tear the earth apart. More than Gunnar's enemies would fall.

"Hallgerd." Gunnar glanced back at me. He looked suddenly tired, like he'd been fighting way too long. That look, too, reminded me of Dad—not Dad when I was younger, but Dad this past year, after Mom had disappeared. Gunnar reached toward my hair, as if to stroke it. I drew away.

"Is it—is it important?" I asked, stalling for time. *Stupid, stupid, stupid.* Of course it was important for Gunnar to restring his bow.

"My life depends on it." He sounded surprised I even needed to ask, and who could blame him? "They'll never defeat me, so long as I have my bow." A cry from below drew him back to the wall, but even as he swung at the next enemy, he gestured toward the bow.

In my head Hallgerd hissed, *"If Gunnar dies, your berserk dies, too."*

Maybe she was lying. Anyone who could kill her first two husbands could lie a little, right? Maybe Ari wasn't even there.

I knew better, though. Of course Ari was there, waiting for me to return. He wouldn't abandon me.

"Free, free, free!" In my head, the fire spirits roared their laughter.

We'd all die if I set those spirits free. The earth would burn, just like in my dreams, down to its very core. This small island would be torn apart. Maybe the rest of the world would suffer, too, if my dreams spoke true.

"The world will end one day whether we will it or no,"

Hallgerd said, as if hearing my thought. *"That's no reason to give up all honor."*

What honor was there in letting the land burn? Yet if Hallgerd hurt Ari—but Ari would die, too, if I set Hallgerd's fire loose into the world. And I'd be throwing away Freki's gift, which had gotten me here.

"I—I can't," I stammered to Gunnar. My throat tightened. I choked out the words. "I won't."

"I'll kill him, Haley!" Hallgerd yelled.

A man leaped right up beside Gunnar. Gunnar struck at the man, through his shield and the arm that held it. The man toppled to the floor, blood gushing from his arm, jagged bones breaking through his skin. Tired as he was, Gunnar was still strong. Maybe he didn't need his bow.

"I'm sorry," I told him. Tears traced hot tracks down my cheeks. "You have no idea."

The look that came over Gunnar's face was beyond describing. It was the look of a man who has seen his death. I thought he'd plead, or take my hair by force. It wasn't like he wasn't strong enough. But he only let out a breath. "Everyone has their own way of being remembered," he said. "I will not ask you again." Gunnar swung at another man, causing him to fall. Then his gaze returned to me, and the strangest expression crossed his face. "What is this, Hallgerd? Your eyes—"

Two men climbed over the edge together. Gunnar whirled away, axe raised, even as I thought, *He knows.*

Gunnar sliced at one man's leg, another man's arm. The men stumbled but kept fighting. A third man came up to fight beside them. I still held my knife, but it was little larger than a steak knife. What use would that be against swords? I sheathed the blade at my belt, stood, and backed away. Splinters from what remained of the roof caught my hair. The wood began to smolder. I quickly ducked away.

I should get out of here, I thought, *before they attack me, too, or worse.* I could run for it, escape down the ladder . . . I didn't. If I couldn't save Gunnar's life, the least I could do was stay and watch. Surely he had other family. They'd want to know what had happened.

Like you can tell anyone anything once you're dead, I thought. But still I waited. I owed him that much.

Gunnar fought for a long time, way longer than I thought possible. Three more men came up into the loft. Gunnar fought them all, spinning from one to another with inhuman speed. His battle cries joined the roar of fire in my ears. Yet in the end he stumbled, and one of them struck a blow to his arm. His axe fell, and another man seized it.

Someone thrust a spear into his chest. Blood bubbled up as that man drew his spear free. Gunnar gave a little gasp and fell. His axe arm twitched, and then he was still, eyes staring at the too-blue sky.

Hallgerd's keening burst into my head, a terrible sound. *She loved him,* I thought numbly. *The story got it wrong. She really loved him.* I fell to my knees and threw up.

I heard footsteps approach me, looked up to see myself surrounded by Gunnar's killers. Their expressions were grim. There was blood on their clothes, and one of them held his arm to his side. *Shit.* I unsheathed the little knife, knowing it couldn't possibly do any good against them all.

One of the men nodded at me, a surprisingly respectful gesture. "Lady," he said. It was hard to hear him over the fire's roaring and Hallgerd's keening. "Will you give us land to bury our dead?"

Was he *serious*? "Fuck off," I told him in English. Then, in Icelandic, "No, I have a better idea. Why don't you dig a hole deep enough to bury you all?"

The men laughed, all but the one who had spoken. "You have reason enough for anger at us," he said soberly. "You have lost much today." He turned away, and the others followed him. Together they tossed their fallen friend over the wall, then climbed down after him. Just like that.

Blood still flowed from Gunnar's chest. I knelt beside him and felt for a pulse, though I knew there was no point. My hands came away sticky with blood.

I hid my face in my burning blond hair, the hair a man had died for, and I wept.

Hallgerd's cries in my head fell silent at last. *"Oh, you have not yet begun to grieve, Haley. I will give you something to weep for. Your knife is sharp enough, I think."*

"No!" I forced myself to my feet and grabbed the coin from the pouch. "Here. You can have it!"

"*What use have I for your gifts now? Keep the life you've destroyed. I may have given over control of the coin and the spell, but its tools—the bowl and the stone and what remains of the blood—lie with me. Until you gather them all again, you cannot cast the spell, not without my consent. And that I will not give. I will not return!*"

The coin flared hotter. "*Free,*" roared the powers Hallgerd had bargained with—the powers I'd bargained with. Against my will I felt my other hand draw the little knife from its sheath. "*Free us,*" the fire spirits roared. "*Free the doubled power you now hold.*"

My tears were fire. My thoughts were fire. Fire surged through my hair, my blood. I touched the wood beneath me, and my fingers left black charred prints behind. "*Free,*" the fire creatures cried. "*We* will *be free.*"

With a sick lurch I knew that refusing Gunnar my hair hadn't been enough. No one could hold so much power for long and live.

This wasn't over yet. It would never be over, not until the fire consumed me after all.

～ *Chapter 17* ～

Somehow I unclenched my hand, and the knife clattered to the floor. I drew my hands into fists, right around the coin. My fingers sought my palms. I had only to break skin, and the fire would leave me, and *I* would be free.

I shut my eyes. I saw a vision of my blood hitting the earth, turning to flame as it landed. I saw earth splitting open around the flames, and a huge fiery hand reaching for the sky.

My skin was burning away from within. The burning *hurt*—but I forced my fists open, dropping the coin. I could handle pain. I'd hold this fire for as long as I could. I opened my eyes. Flames still danced before me. My hands went right through them, as if they were ghosts.

"*Shall I let you know,*" Hallgerd said, her voice high and taunting, "*the moment my blade breaks his skin?*"

"Please," I begged Hallgerd, because I knew there was no reasoning with the fire inside me.

Hallgerd's laughter in my head was a wild thing. "*Would you bargain with me? What compensation can you possibly offer for Gunnar's life?*"

"You have my mother's life." My voice grew wild as hers. "Isn't that enough?"

"*There's no such thing as enough, not anymore. He flinches quite nicely, Haley. Even so, he says you should not listen to me. Foolish boy. Do you think whether Haley listens or not matters to me anymore?*"

I clutched the broken roof with my free hand, but drew away when it began smoldering again. In the distance below, from the smaller outbuildings that surrounded this one, people—servants?—began making their way nervously outside. Closer by, Gunnar's killers were indeed silently digging holes for their dead, while an old woman shouted at them, cussing up a blue streak.

"She refused him her hair," one of the gravediggers said. He laughed. "Did you hear? She is a bad woman, that one."

As if *they* hadn't wanted him dead. As if they hadn't struck the blows that killed him. I moved closer to the edge. I swayed, dizzy a moment, ghost flames all around me.

"*Jump,*" the fire in me roared. "*Jump.*"

"*Yes,*" Hallgerd agreed. "*Why not jump? What's left for you to lose?*"

"Only this island," I whispered. "Only the world."

"*What good has the world ever done either of us?*"

No. You didn't destroy the whole world because your own life was messed up. I stepped away from the edge, though it would have been easy—too easy—to set the fire loose.

Down below, a young woman rode up on horseback, taking in the men and the old woman with a glance. The old woman cursed at her, too. The young woman ignored her, dismounted, dropped the horse's reins, and ran for the house. I heard her footsteps on the ladder below. "Mama?" she called, her voice tight with concern.

I turned slowly around. She climbed up into the loft, her wool riding cloak wrapped tight around her. A few blond strands fell loose from beneath her hood. She was younger than Hallgerd, older than me, with a stubborn set to her chin. My throat tightened as I realized who she must be. Thorgerd. Hallgerd's daughter.

In my head, Hallgerd caught her breath. "*I told her to stay home. I told her to stay safe.*"

Thorgerd's gray eyes swept over the loft to where Gunnar lay. Her father?—no, she'd called herself someone else's daughter in the spellbook. Even so, she let out a little sigh. "It is over, then." She walked over to Gunnar, knelt beside him, and gently shut his eyes. When she stood there was blood on her skirt. "I'm sorry, Mama." She held out her hands to me. Strong hands—unlike mine, they didn't shake.

She's lost her mother, too. She just doesn't know it yet. I took her hands—though mine were still stained with Gunnar's blood—not knowing what else to do. Her skin felt cool against mine.

"So warm," Thorgerd muttered. "You're always warm, Mama, but today—" She drew me into a fierce hug. As I awkwardly hugged her back, I felt something leap from me to her, like a small electric shock. A trickle of the fire beneath my skin left me.

I drew sharply away. The phantom flames faded to bright afterimages, as if I'd looked too long into the sun. The roaring in my ears subsided to a whisper.

"If you dare to hurt her—" Hallgerd left the thought unfinished.

"Of course I wouldn't hurt her!" I wouldn't let the fire in me touch Thorgerd or anyone else if I could help it.

"Whom do you speak to? Your eyes—they are not my mother's eyes." Thorgerd's gaze narrowed. "What thievery is this? Who are you?"

I looked down, unwilling to meet that gaze. I'd stolen her mother, even if I hadn't meant to, just like Hallgerd had stolen mine. Not that losing Hallgerd was all that great a loss.

"Haley!" There was pain in Hallgerd's voice. *"I have never harmed my daughter. What do you take me for?"*

"You killed my mother," I said.

"*It was not my—*" Hallgerd's voice fell silent.

Thorgerd pressed her lips together. "Sorcery." She reached beneath her cloak for something—a knife?—then thought better of it. Her face hardened. "I know well enough my mother meddled with forces beyond this world. She did what she could to shelter me from them, but true dreams run in our family. She could only hide so much."

Heat was building in me again, flames flickering at the edges of my sight. Sweat trickled beneath my dress. "I'm sorry."

"Sorrow serves no one. Tell me what we need to do to call her back."

I glanced at Gunnar's lifeless body. "I don't think she wants to come back."

In my head, I could *feel* Hallgerd's listening silence.

Thorgerd made a dismissive sound. "My mother is many things, but a coward is not one of them."

"*Haley. Give me the coin.*" Hallgerd's words were careful, measured. "*I would leave you to your fate—do not doubt it—but I'll not abandon my daughter. Return my life to me, and I'll return yours to you. Let that serve as compensation enough for the lives we've both taken.*"

I'd had no choice. I didn't owe her any compensation—maybe that didn't matter. Maybe she'd thought she had no choice, too. The air before me wavered. The roaring grew loud again, so loud. What would happen once the fire burst through my skin?

Even in my own time, that fire might destroy me yet. I could stay here. I could make Hallgerd's daughter suffer as I'd suffered, knowing her mother was stolen from her— no. I couldn't. Just like I couldn't leave Ari and Jared—and Dad—to wonder forever what had happened to me.

"You're right," I told Thorgerd, though I could barely hear my own voice over the roaring. "Your mother is no coward." I fumbled for the coin I'd dropped.

"Wait." Thorgerd took my hands again. I felt more fire flowing from me to her. When she pulled her hands away, the heat beneath my skin had cooled a little more. At my startled look, Thorgerd smiled. "I know more of sorcery than my mother thinks. I would have taken some of the fire from her years ago, if only she'd let me. I am sorry I cannot take more." She laid her hand on my shoulder. "Go now. Return to your own place, and give my mother back to me."

"Thank you." I picked up the coin. To Hallgerd I said, "Swear to me you won't set your fire loose once I'm gone, not if you can help it."

Hallgerd laughed bitterly. *"You control the spell. The fire follows you, not me. I give up much because of you, Haley."*

Too much fire—but better that fire stay with me than remain behind with Hallgerd. I would at least try to control it, and I still wasn't sure Hallgerd would. I drew my hand back to throw the coin.

The air blurred before me, and I saw the path once more. Far away, at the end of that path, I saw a girl—myself, only my eyes were gray, not brown—kneeling before the bowl of Freki's blood and chanting.

Not really me. Hallgerd. She reached out her hand.

"A gift!" I called, and threw the coin to her. The path came into sharper focus. On it I saw Thorgerd's daughters and granddaughters and great-granddaughters. The path branched—not all Thorgerd's descendants were my ancestors—but the branches that didn't lead to me disappeared into the distance.

Sunlight glinted off the burning silver as it flew. Hallgerd caught the coin, and that light shone through her fingers.

"Goodbye, Haley. I leave you to your life, and I return to what remains of mine."

The light pulled me along the path, and the fire beneath my skin came with me, all of it, flaring hotter once more. My skin seemed suddenly thin, my hair and limbs and thoughts all made of fire. For a heartbeat I knew the fire would destroy me and burn through to the wide world, right here, right now. But then a green-eyed girl—Thorgerd's daughter—grabbed my hands as I passed her. A spark of fire leaped from me to her. An older woman with a long blond braid did the same, and then another woman with tangled curls falling into her face.

One by one they held out their hands, all of my ancestors, each of them taking a spark—or more than a spark—of power from me, bleeding the fire away. How did they know?

Take some of the fire if you can, but do not take too much. Thorgerd had told them so, in her spellbook. For a thousand years she and her descendants had passed down everything I'd need. Hallgerd must have told her daughter what had happened after all—or maybe Thorgerd had figured it out. *True dreams run in our family.*

The roaring turned to anger. *"Free!"* the fire spirits screamed. *"How dare you deny us? We would be free!"*

I felt the fire in me slowly lessen from the firestorm it was to a mere bonfire. The roaring in my ears—the voices of the fire creatures—turned to whispers. I still burned hot, too hot, but the fire was only enough to destroy me now, not the world around me.

"Thank you," I told each of my ancestors in turn. "Thank you."

My own grandmother's grandmother took my hands, taking a spark of my fire. Almost enough—but the bonfire burned on. My great-grandmother and grandmother looked at me with confusion, concern—but they'd grown up thousands of miles from Thorgerd and her warnings. They took nothing from me.

"We cannot have the world," the fire spirits whispered, *"but we can destroy you. We will destroy you."*

Fire caressed my face, my arms, my hair. It didn't hurt anymore, which scared me more than any pain. *At least the fire will consume only me.*

The last woman on the path looked up at me—or maybe she'd never stopped looking. My mother's gray eyes grew wide. *Please, please don't let her see me die.*

She dropped what she was holding—a coin, the same coin I'd held, only she'd caught it a year before I had—and ran to me. The fire seemed to fade as my mother drew me close. I clung to her, inhaling the scent of her hair, remembering how it felt to be safe in her arms. "Mom. I missed you so much."

"Haley, how on earth—" Mom stroked my hair, drew back, and touched my face. "Honey, you're burning up." She grabbed my hands.

"Mom, no!"

Too late—fire flowed from me to her, fast and fierce. Mom hadn't read Thorgerd's warnings, either. She didn't know not to take too much. Or maybe she did know. I tried to pull away, but she wouldn't let go. She drew me closer instead.

It happened so fast, flames leaping at her arms and legs and hair. In moments she turned to ashes in my arms, leaving only the faintest spark of fire behind. "Mom!"

I fell to my knees with a gasp, and my eyes flew open. My hands were covered with fox blood, and a smooth silver coin lay in my palm. The pattern etched upon it was gone, the magic spent at last. Water dripped from the gray sky and my wet hair, dimpling the surface of the blood in the bowl. Most of that blood was gone now; only enough remained to cover the stone. Wind blew, and I shivered, feeling the cold down to my bones.

Ari stared down at me, a knife in one hand and a blue LED flashlight in the other. "Haley?" he asked, but his voice was uncertain.

I let the coin fall to the grass, where Freki's limp body still lay. The fox's open eyes reminded me of Gunnar. Thinking of Thorgerd, I closed them, then looked up at Ari. "Yeah, Luke," I said, in English so there could be no doubt. "It's me."

"Oh, good," Ari said in Icelandic. He fell to his knees as well. "I wasn't sure I could keep that up much longer. Hallgerd was distracted, I don't know why, but I got the knife away from her, and then she didn't like the flashlight any more than Svan did, only after that she said she was leaving, so I let her say the spell and—are you all right, Haley?"

I shook my head. "Mom." My voice came out as a shuddering sob. "She's gone."

"Oh," Ari said softly. He set down the knife and took me into his arms. I buried my head against his jacket. It smelled faintly of seawater and of bear. Cool tears flowed down my face. "Mom didn't *know*. She took too much fire. I couldn't stop her."

Ari didn't try to tell me everything was all right. He

didn't even ask what I was talking about. He just held me as I cried on and the rain drizzled all around us. *What is the fate of the world, against this one life?*

The sound of wingbeats made us both stiffen. I drew away slowly. Ari took my hand, and we got to our feet as Muninn landed in the wet grass in front of us. The little black-and-white terns landed beside him, and then came a second raven who watched us thoughtfully but said nothing. I looked down into Muninn's small dark eyes. Did my human life mean anything more to him than to his master? Did Mom's? "You can't take my memories anymore." I kept my voice steady, though I still felt tear-tracks on my cheeks. "So what do you want with me?"

Muninn's wings beat the air. "Only to offer my thanks. You have done better than I expected, Haley, Amanda and Gabriel's daughter, and so this land will hold a time longer. I shall return to it all its memories of you. I trust you will accept that as payment for my misjudging you?"

The salty taste of my tears reminded me of a piece of licorice, offered freely by a girl who thought I was a ghost. I was so tired of every gift having a price. "Just make sure you give back the land's memories of me and Ari both."

"Very well." Muninn lifted his beak toward Ari. "So long as I am dispensing gifts, do you wish to forget your warrior ancestors once more?"

Ari hesitated, then shook his head. "No. Only—I would like to get to decide when to change, if I may."

Muninn threw his head back, and the glint in his eyes was like laughter. "You need only remove the jacket for that." The laughter died as he stalked past us to where Freki's body lay. The other raven followed him. They stared at the fox, their wings utterly still, and then Muninn tipped the driftwood bowl over with his beak.

Freki's blood steamed as it soaked into the earth, much as the mead of poetry once had. The blood on my hands steamed, too. That steam stung my eyes, and I blinked. When I opened them again, my hands were clean and Freki was gone.

Both ravens launched into the sky, and the little birds followed them.

"Have a care," Muninn's wingbeats said as he disappeared into the clouds. "If we both have good fortune, we will not meet again."

Cold rain soaked through my sodden jeans and jacket. Ari and I watched, still holding hands, as the birds disappeared out of sight. Only then did I realize that the mead skin was gone, as well as Hallgerd's coin. The spell was done, I thought, the coin blank. Muninn didn't need it— but even ordinary ravens liked shiny things.

The sound of a car on the gravel lane made us jump. A door slammed, then another. Katrin came running up the hillside, a notebook clutched in one hand. She stopped short when she saw us, as if she couldn't believe we were real. "You're all right?" she asked in Icelandic.

"For certain definitions of all right, yeah," Ari said, also in Icelandic. A wry smile tugged at his face. Katrin ran forward, dropped the notebook, and grabbed him in her arms. "Thank God," she whispered, then drew away and took my hands.

The last spark of fire in me leaped at her touch, and some small splinter of that spark passed from me to her. "I would have taken it all," Katrin said, in English now. Rain made strands of her flyaway hair stick to her face. "I was hoping—to cast the spell, and take your mother's fire, and set things right."

I said nothing. For just a moment, I wished Katrin could have taken the fire instead of Mom, too. But then Ari broke in in Icelandic with, "Oh, yeah, because that would have been *so* much better," and I knew I didn't mean it. I never, ever wanted Ari to miss his mother like I missed mine.

"It's okay," I said in English, though of course it wasn't. "It's—it's over, anyway." That was a start. But I felt more sobs rising within me. "I lost her," I said, trying to keep the sobs inside as once I'd tried to contain a blazing fire. "I lost everything."

"Not everything," a strangled voice said.

I looked up. My father stood a short distance down the hill, his hair sticking out in every direction, his jacket dripping rainwater. He looked like he might shatter into a million pieces if he took a single step.

Or maybe that was me. My legs shook as I drew away

from Katrin and walked to him. Dad grabbed me in his arms, holding me so tightly I could barely breathe. I wouldn't have pulled away for the world, though. More tears came, the tears I'd spent a year trying to hide from him.

"I thought I'd lost you both," Dad said.

I heard the whisper of wingbeats in the air. Dad heard it, too, and we both fell silent.

"I will remember her, Haley," Muninn said, just before he slipped out of hearing. "I remember all who live here, always."

~ *Chapter 18* ~

It was because of Jared that Dad and Katrin had found us.

For three months they'd searched, Katrin insisting there was magic involved, Dad not believing her. Then Muninn's spell kicked in, leaving Dad wondering why he'd stayed in Iceland so long, and leaving Katrin with an apartment full of pictures she couldn't quite focus on and an entire room she kept finding reasons not to enter.

But then Jared called Dad, who said of course he didn't have a daughter. So Jared tried Katrin, whose phone number Dad had given him the day we disappeared, before he'd gotten an Iceland-friendly cell phone. Katrin didn't remember us, either, but she remembered Thorgerd's spell for restoring lost memories. Somehow, she convinced Dad to cast the spell with her.

It took them a while to get all the supplies—you can't exactly buy raven feathers at the mall—but in the end the spell worked, and they headed straight for Hlidarendi. Dad drove while Katrin pored over the spellbook, hoping she'd get there in time to cast the spell instead of me.

They explained all of this as Katrin drove us back to Reykjavik and Ari and I wolfed down the hot dogs we'd picked up from a gas station along the way. Or rather from a grill set up outside the gas station—everyone was outside again, because of the earthquake at Hlidarendi this time, and we passed several more emergency vehicles.

"It was awful," Dad said—meaning Muninn's spell, not the earthquake. He glanced back at me, as if to make sure I was still there. "I knew I'd lost something important, only I couldn't figure out what." Beside him, Katrin's hands tightened on the wheel.

It was already midafternoon. Time always seemed to get away from me when Muninn was around. I thought of my run by the harbor, of how I'd heard a raven's cry and the beating of wings. Like all the other time I'd lost, those six hours had been Muninn's fault, not Hallgerd's.

Once the hot dogs were gone, Ari fell asleep in the backseat, his head resting on my shoulder. I saw Dad watching us again; Dad saw me watching him and quickly looked away. I stroked Ari's hair, which felt *just* like bear fur, and wondered what on earth I was going to tell Jared when I called him.

*   *   *

Flosi threw himself at Ari the instant we opened the door to his apartment, before he could even pull off his shoes. The quake hadn't reached as far as Reykjavik, so it was safe to go inside. Once the sheepdog had gotten his entire wriggling body into Ari's lap on the couch, it was Ari's and my turn to explain.

We told Dad and Katrin everything, in English for Dad's benefit. They listened, not saying a word, though Katrin's arms gripped her chair and Dad ran his hands through his hair so many times I was sure it would never lie flat again.

Neither of them spoke when we were through, either, not for long moments. Then Dad turned, slowly, to Katrin. "There was a time," he told her, "when I said that you were crazy. I'd like to take that back now, if I may."

"And I as well," Ari said. Flosi had fallen asleep in his lap, and Ari absently scratched the dog's ears.

Katrin shut her eyes, as if their apologies pained her. "I wish I had been crazy, and that none of this had happened. I wish—" She looked at Dad; he looked at her. They didn't look like they hated each other anymore. They looked more like—not lovers. Like old friends who'd been through the same war together. The war in which their children were lost and found again.

"I'm sorry," I said. "I never should have run. If I hadn't run, Mom might not—"

"Haley." Dad's voice was quiet as I'd ever heard it. "This is not your fault. If anyone is to blame—" He buried his face in his hands. "It's me, Haley."

"Not only you," Katrin said.

"Oh sure, let's all fight over whose fault it is," Ari said. "Can I have a turn, too?" Flosi stirred in his lap and let out a single woof. "See? Even Flosi wants his chance at feeling guilty." Ari pressed his face into the dog's fur. His shoulders shook, laughing or sobbing, I couldn't tell.

Katrin watched him, her expression strange. "You were really a bear?"

"Oh, yeah, that reminds me." Ari's shaking stilled as he nudged Flosi from his lap and took off his jacket. "You don't want a bear in the apartment. They run around, break all the furniture—it is a problem. For now, I will be human."

Katrin gave a shaky laugh, but Dad only sighed and ran his hands through his hair once more. "Just like us all," he said.

The sun was down and Ari and I were yawning by the time Katrin drove Dad and me back to the guesthouse. Along the way Dad and Katrin told us how the earthquakes in the Westfjords had lots of people confused, while the quake at Hlidarendi had them worried because of all the volcanoes nearby. There'd be no more earthquakes because of my magic, or Hallgerd's, either, but no one knew that yet. At least no one was seriously hurt, in either place, because Icelanders built for quakes. I guess you do that when your home is one big geologic event waiting to happen.

In the car, Flosi gave my hands a thorough licking over. His nose got under Ari's handkerchief bandage and it fell away, revealing the puckered skin below. I handed the handkerchief to Ari, but he shook his head. "Keep it. You never know when you'll hurt yourself again."

He meant it as a joke, but I glanced at the scars on my palms, then back at my burned wrist. I remembered the fire that had burst through my skin, and I shook my head. "I'm done with that," I said, but I kept his handkerchief anyway.

When we reached the guesthouse, Ari and I looked at each other, suddenly a little uncomfortable, neither of us sure what to say.

"You still owe me a song," I said at last, and turned away before Ari could see my eyes stinging. I hurried after Dad into the guesthouse.

By the time Dad and I got inside, I wanted nothing more than to sleep for a week, but there was something I had to know first. "Were you and Mom really planning a divorce?"

Dad let out a breath, and something of the old lost look returned to his face. But I waited, and finally he looked right at me and said, "I don't know, Haley. I honestly don't."

"Did you talk about getting one?"

"No. That was my first mistake, not talking to your mother. I'm not always much good at talking—I guess you know that. Maybe we could have worked things out. I don't *know*." He reached into his pocket and pulled out his phone. "Here. You should let Jared know you're okay."

I was so tired. I couldn't deal with Jared now. "I'll call him in the morning, I—"

"Don't be like me," Dad said. "Talk to him. Don't worry about the charges. Take as long as you need."

Jared picked up on the first ring. "Haley?" The strained hope in his voice nearly broke my heart.

"Yeah. It's me."

"You're not going to disappear again?"

"No," I promised him. "It's over."

I told Jared everything, too, crying all over again as I did. Talking to him felt good. I realized just how much I'd missed him.

We talked for a really long time.

I had no idea what time it was when I finally fell into bed. I barely had time to grab Mortimer—he wasn't a bear, but he'd do—before I fell asleep.

I dreamed I walked on a green summer hillside, dandelions blooming, gulls circling up above. There was no fire, just a gently trickling stream and a distant figure walking toward me. As the figure drew closer, I recognized her. "Mom!"

She smiled and reached for me. Yet as our hands met, flames flared between us. Mom turned to hot ash, sifting like snow through my fingers. I would have screamed then, only the fire had burned my voice away. I ran, knowing any moment I would burn, too.

But I didn't. A cool breeze caressed my neck, and I found myself jogging along a path beside a harbor. The sky above shone with stars. When I looked down, I saw a white fox running by my side.

"At least now I know what happened," I said to him. "That's something, isn't it?"

Freki didn't answer. He just cocked an ear in my direction as we ran on, the little fox keeping me company through the rest of the night, clear on to morning.

Wind gusted as Dad and I walked between the blocky stone walls of Thingvellir two days later. Rain spat from the sky, and I shivered in my jacket. The wind felt good, though. I didn't think I'd ever mind the cold again.

We stopped when we reached the Law Rock, and together we stared out at the river. The geese were gone now, leaving behind grasses that blazed bright shades of orange and red. Most of the tourists had left, too. Only a few people walked the path behind us.

"So this is where it happened," I said.

Dad turned to look at me, his eyes damp. "I miss her, Haley. You know that, don't you?"

I nodded, not trusting myself to speak. *Either you loved someone or you didn't.* Was it ever that simple?

Dad shoved his hands into his pockets. "Can you ever forgive me?"

My throat hurt, but I forced myself to speak. "I'm working on it," I said, and meant it.

We walked back down the path in silence, to the Hotel Valholl, where we were meeting Ari and Katrin for dinner. Ari and I had slept most of yesterday away. We'd seen each other only briefly, when Dad and Katrin brought us to the police station to file a report. Apparently the police had thought it might have been Dad and Katrin's fault we'd disappeared, that maybe they'd abducted us or something, and Mom before us, too. They seemed to believe Ari's and my story that we'd run away, though, right down to our claiming that Ari had dyed his hair and I'd cut mine to make us harder to recognize.

Ari looked up from the newspaper he was reading as we entered the room. His leather jacket was replaced by fleece-lined black nylon, along with a bleached wool cap almost as pale as his hair. "Hey," he said in English. "It says here they found a staff carved with magical runes in the

Westfjords. Very mysterious, no sign of the owner. The people at the Sorcery Museum are looking into it."

"There's a *sorcery* museum?" I said, also in English, as I slid into my seat.

"Yeah. In Holmavik. Too bad we forgot to visit. Of course, we were a bit busy."

"Just a bit." I turned to the menu, which was written in both English and Icelandic. I read the English, then ordered in Icelandic, which seemed to startle the waiter. Even if I spoke the language, a million other small things gave me away as the foreigner I was.

"It's going to take a while to get used to that," Dad said. "I bet you could place out of your language requirement when we get home, though."

I switched to English automatically. "Yeah, because that would make it all totally worth it, right?" I managed a laugh.

Katrin glanced at Ari's white hair. "We all have things to get used to." She spoke English, too. She sipped her coffee and looked at Dad and me over the rim of her cup. "You've decided to go back, then?"

Ari looked down, suddenly very interested in his napkin. I nodded slowly. "There still might be time to catch up at school. Keep me from losing the year." *Give Dad and me a chance to learn how to live alone with each other.*

"I wish you would stay," Katrin said. "Not all the stories

about Hallgerd and Thorgerd are written down. I'd tell you the rest of what was passed on to me."

"Nah, Jared would be disappointed if she didn't come home," Ari said.

I looked sharply over at him. Ari met my gaze. "Hey, two days ago we were not sure we would make it back at all. It is good that you can go home."

I kept looking at him. "Want to go for a walk?" I said.

"It is freezing out there. Why would anyone—I am being stupid again. Yes, I would love to go for a walk."

I glanced at Dad, and he nodded. Ari followed me out.

As we headed across the parking lot and onto the path, something icy blew into our faces. I held out my hand, and a cold flake landed there. Snow.

Back home, they were still having hundred-degree days. Even without magic, I'd be warm soon enough. The thought wasn't as comforting as it should have been. I missed the desert, but I was going to miss Iceland, too. Would it always be like this, wishing for whichever place I couldn't be? "Dad says maybe we can come back for Christmas," I told Ari in Icelandic.

"The weather's worse at Christmas," Ari said, also in Icelandic. "More snow, and it's dark all the time. Of course you don't want to stay."

I stopped and stared at a cluster of bright red flowers. Didn't they know that it was way too cold to bloom? "I talked to Jared."

Ari didn't look at me. "I'm sure he's glad you're okay."

"Of course he's glad. Jared's my best friend. He's been worried sick these past months. He wants to know what it's like to be a bear, too, by the way. I think he's a little jealous of you."

Ari gave a wry laugh. "We're even there, then."

"You're not listening!" Or maybe I wasn't saying it right. "I told Jared how much I'd missed him. And I told him how much I was going to miss you."

Ari opened his mouth as if to make a joke, shut it again. Around us the snow kept falling.

I drew a deep breath. *Either you loved someone or you didn't.* But what if you loved more than one person? Or what if things changed? "We decided—we're only sixteen, okay? Maybe in Hallgerd's time that was old enough to be married off whether you wanted to be or not, but neither of us wants to live out some ancient tragedy. We're not ready to decide about the rest of our lives, you know?" I was having enough trouble getting through each day right now. I'd had more nightmares last night.

"So you're—"

"We're not breaking up."

"No, of course not," Ari said, a little too fast. "I didn't mean—"

"But we're both going to see other people, too."

Any clever comeback Ari had died on his lips. He stared at me in complete silence.

I was suddenly very aware of how close we were standing. "I mean, assuming you're okay with that"—I was the one talking too fast now—"because maybe you're not and I'd totally understand if—"

Ari leaned forward and kissed me.

I kissed him back. His hands were warm against my neck. I pulled off his hat, running my own hands through his soft hair. The *Star Wars* theme blared from Ari's pocket, but we ignored it. His lips were soft, too, and his skin smelled faintly of snow and more faintly of bear, and the heat that rose in me had nothing at all to do with magic.

"Yes, Haley," Ari said when we pulled apart at last. "I'm okay with that." He smiled. No matter what happened a year, five years from now, I would always love that smile. "Are you leaving right away?"

"Next week. Dad couldn't get a flight out any sooner."

"Good," Ari said. "Because your song, it isn't finished yet."

My song? "You didn't have to write something new for me." But I smiled, too.

"No, I wanted to, only—I don't like the ending anymore. Too much of that ancient tragedy stuff. I want to change it, but I wasn't sure you'd be here long enough."

The snow fell harder, white flakes landing on Ari's pale eyelashes. His cell phone rang once more. I put my arms around his neck and looked right into his bright green eyes.

"I have time," I said.

⌁ Author's Note ⌁

Hallgerd, Gunnar, Thorgerd, Svan, Hrut, and Hallgerd's father, Hoskuld, are all found in the pages of *Njal's Saga,* one of the best-known and best-loved of the Icelandic sagas—medieval stories about Iceland's early inhabitants. It is likely Hallgerd and her kin really existed, but all the rest is uncertain. Although *Njal's Saga* took place a thousand years ago, it wasn't written down until the thirteenth century, and as a result it's hard to know which events are real and which aren't, or exactly where history ends and fiction begins.

Many of the details in *Thief Eyes* come directly from *Njal's Saga:* that Hallgerd's uncle Svan was a sorcerer and her uncle Hrut could see the future, that Hrut said Hallgerd had the eyes of a thief, the deaths of Hallgerd's husbands, and—most memorably—Hallgerd's refusing Gunnar two locks of her hair. Other details are my own invention: that Hallgerd studied sorcery with Svan, that Thorgerd inherited Hrut's gift of prophecy, and that Thorgerd had any daughters, let alone daughters whose descendants live on today. None of these things directly contradict the saga, but none of them appear in its pages, either.

Berserks get little mention in *Njal's Saga*, but *Egil's Saga* features a shape-shifting wolf. In general there are more references to berserks turning into wolves than into bears, but as Freki says, no wolf has ever set foot on Iceland's shores. Many of the sagas mention sorcery, but they give few details about how it was practiced. The Museum of Icelandic Sorcery and Witchcraft has more extensive records of spells and spellbooks from later times, though. Hallgerd's spell was inspired by these records, but it, too, is ultimately my invention.

Freki, Muninn, the fire giants, and the mead of poetry come not from the sagas but from Norse mythology. Freki and Muninn are companions to the Norse god Odin—their master, whom Ari refuses to name—and Freki, too, is traditionally a wolf. Muninn has always been a raven, but I invented his mountain—although there *is* a mountain in Iceland's Westfjords—Kaldbakshorn—into which *Njal's Saga* says Svan may have disappeared when he died. The voices in Muninn's mountain are loosely based on several other sagas, as well as (once Haley and Ari begin to climb) a few bits of later Icelandic history. The woman whose lover refuses to take her abroad is Gudrun from *Laxdaela Saga*.

If you'd like to read *Njal's Saga, Egil's Saga, Laxdaela Saga,* or any of the other Icelandic sagas, I recommend finding a relatively recent print translation; in my experience, contemporary translations tend to be more accessible and readable than the older public domain translations available online. For *Njal's Saga,* I enjoyed both the Robert Cook and Lee M. Hollander translations.

Finally, most of the places Haley and Ari visit are real, and many still bear the names they held a thousand years ago. Hoskuldsstadir, Hrutsstadir, and Svansholl are all named for their original owners and remain working farms today. Hlidarendi, the hillside where Gunnar died, also kept its saga-era name and is now the site of a parish church. And Thingvellir, the original site of Iceland's Althing, or parliament, probably appears in more Icelandic sagas than any other location.

This book began at Thingvellir. As I walked through that rift valley for the first time, a half-read copy of *Njal's Saga* in my backpack, I heard a woman's voice whisper in my head, low and full of rage, *"I will not allow it."* Later, I would wonder where that voice came from and whether it was real. Right then, I knew only that I had to stop, sit down, and write down Hallgerd's words and the opening scene of *Thief Eyes.*

~ *Acknowledgments* ~

Many thanks to:

Sigurður Atlason, manager of the Museum of Icelandic Sorcery and Witchcraft, and Björk Bjarnadóttir, environmental ethnologist, for answering my many questions and making me feel welcome in the Strandir region. Lárus Bragason, for a tour of the *Njal's Saga* sites in the south of Iceland, where Hallgerd, Gunnar, and their neighbors lived. Matthias Johannsson of the Hótel Laugarhóll for the best meal I had in Iceland, with apologies for sending an earthquake to his hotel in return. Wildlife biologist Andrew Trent for answering my questions about polar bears. Stephanie Rosas, William Winhall, and Kelly Terry of Sea-World San Diego for not only answering my questions but also letting me visit with their resident arctic foxes, Boris and Natasha.

Inga Þóra Ingvarsdóttir for reading the manuscript from an Icelander's perspective, for answering more questions, and for always being willing to geek out about the sagas with me. Sarah Johnson and her daughter Elayne for reading the manuscript from the perspective of Americans living in Iceland, and all their family for welcoming us into their home. Everyone else who read all or part of the manuscript, sometimes on short notice: C. S. Adler, Catherine Keegan, Jill Knowles, Larry Hammer, Ann Manheimer, Patricia McCord, Earl Parrish, Frances Robertson, and Jennifer J. Stewart. My husband, Larry Hammer, again, because it was his idea to go to Iceland in the first place, and because his memory for visual details—not to mention his quiet conviction that of course I could write this book—helped me through countless scenes.

My fabulous editor at Random House, Jim Thomas, who always knows how to make my words better, as well as Random House editorial assistant Chelsea Eberly, publicist Meg O'Brien, and designer Heather Palisi, all of whom have helped to get those words out into the world.

My also-fabulous agent, Nancy Gallt, and her assistant, Marietta Zacker.

With so many people doing so much to help me, any mistakes that remain must be my own. Thank you all. I couldn't have written this one without you.

Don't miss Janni Lee Simner's
sequel to *Bones of Faerie*!

Faerie Winter

"Ethan!" My voice tightened around the call. I couldn't let him go. I had to know why he was afraid, and whether his magic had truly killed, and, if it had, how likely it was to kill again. *"Ethan, stop!"*

He jerked to a stop, just as I'd commanded. I felt the cold thread of my magic stretching between us.

Fear crept into his eyes. "You did that before, too, didn't you? Just like she did."

"Like who did?" I walked past Ethan, putting myself between him and the stairs. Matthew followed with the water basin.

"Let me go." Smoke rose from Ethan's bandages. "Let me go or I'll *kill* you, I swear it."

"Liza." There was a warning in Matthew's voice.

I ignored it, keeping my gaze and my magic focused on Ethan. "Like you killed Ben?"

Flames burst through Ethan's bandages. The magic binding him to me burned away as charred linen drifted to the floor. The boy drew his hands together, cupping a ball of fire within.

Matthew flung the water at him. The fire hissed but didn't go out. The scent of damp coals filled the air.

Matthew held the basin in front of us like a shield. "Easy, Ethan. We won't hurt you."

"*You* won't, maybe." Ethan's dark eyes reflected the fire he held. I felt its heat against my skin. Flames cast light onto the basin Matthew held. Brightness filled my sight— *No. Not now.* This was no time for visions. I tried to turn away, but it was too late. I had no choice but to see—

Cloaked figures following a river toward a town. One of them—a girl my age in a cloak the bright green of mulberry leaves—hesitated a moment, drawing back her hood to reveal long clear hair and bright silver eyes. Faerie eyes, I thought, and then I saw—

Flames consuming the town's houses. Snow sizzled as burning timbers crashed to the ground. Smoke billowed up and I saw—

Ethan watching the houses burn, the clear-haired girl's hand on his arm. She smiled at him, and he smiled back. Neither of them moved to stop the flames. Neither did the younger children arrayed around them. Those flames burned brighter, and by their glow I saw—

Fire leaping from cupped hands to catch at a door-frame. Heat pulsed against my clothes and skin as wood burned—

Metal clattered as the basin hit the ground. Matthew grabbed my arm, and I realized these flames came from no vision. They were real, and they wreathed the doorway to Mom's room.